The Ghost Girl

"When I grow up, I'm going to leave Ireland," I told the Canon, when we got in the house.

"Oh no," he said. "You stay."

"Why should I?" I asked.

"Because somebody's got to see both sides," he said . . .

There's a fierce bit of me that doesn't want to go, because it is my land. I've as much right to it as all the people in the secret armies, with all their fancy initials, going around scrawling their names on graves . . .

Catherine Sefton's Donegal ghost story
binds the reader with its
haunting quality while also putting the current situation
in Ireland
into a historical perspective.

Also by Catherine Sefton
in Magnet Books

The Sleepers on the Hill
Emer's Ghost
The Emma Dilemma
The Island of the Strangers

The
Ghost Girl

CATHERINE SEFTON

A Magnet Book

For
Kathleen Morgan
and
May O'Friel
with apologies to the bungalow!

First published in Great Britain 1985
by Hamish Hamilton Children's Books
Magnet paperback edition first published 1986
by Methuen Children's Books Limited
11 New Fetter Lane, London EC4P 4EE
Text copyright © Catherine Sefton
Reproduced, printed and bound in Great Britain by
Hazell Watson & Viney Limited,
Member of the BPCC Group,
Aylesbury, Bucks

ISBN 0 416 61530 9

1

My name is Clare Campbell and I'm the one who saw the ghost.

I wouldn't be writing about it, but the Canon said I should, if only to get it out of my system. I don't know whether he believes me about the ghost bit, but he had to believe the rest, because I worked it out. It was like being a detective, some of it, and it all made sense. The Canon agrees about that.

I'll begin with the ghost . . . the first time I saw her, that is.

I'd been out walking Maxie, that's my brother. We were staying in this guest house. My Dad had his business burnt out. It was a shop, and some rotten nerk put a petrol bomb in it. We were sick, and Dad said we should clear off and have a holiday to forget it.

That's what Dad said we were doing anyway, but it wasn't really. The thing is, he was fed up with the Irish troubles, and what happened at the end was that he and Mum went to Scotland to see if he could get a shop there, and start up again where there wouldn't be I.R.A. men burning things. They left us up in Bonecastle,

1

where we were supposed to enjoy ourselves, but it was a bit difficult because every time we went down the street we saw 'Brits Out' signs and things. There are a lot of I.R.A. men in Bonecastle, because it is just over the border in the Republic, and makes a good hidey hole for them to go raiding on our side. They haven't got round to burning the Bonecastle shops yet.

My sister Mo didn't want to come to Bonecastle because of *them*, but my Dad said he didn't want to farm us out to strangers and he was as Irish as the I.R.A. any day, even if he was a Protestant, sort of, and he wasn't going to let the Provos chase us off. He went to *look* in Scotland, but he came back, and now we're rebuilding the shop, right where the old one was.

Anyway, Mo cheered up when she got to Bonecastle, because she found a Mystery Man, and that left me minding Maxie in Garrison House, and feeling very fed up. I wish Mo had never discovered boyfriends.

That's what I was thinking about when I went up to our room, and then the whole world suddenly went upside down!

I opened the door, and *she* was there.

"Who . . ." I said, and then I stopped, because I knew she wasn't real.

She was bigger than me, about Mo sized. She didn't move or say or do anything. She just stood there, by the window, gazing at me, but not really *at* me. I don't believe she could see me at all.

She was stiff, and still, and in a funny way almost colourless, drained. She was like a wax-work, except that you can't see through wax-works, and I could see through her. I could see the curtains, and the wall, just before she faded into it.

The wall swallowed her up. I had the idea that she'd come out of it, somehow, and now she just faded back in, through the crummy old rose and petal wallpaper.

So that was my ghost girl!

2

I was scared stiff!

I'd never seen anything like that before.

I don't know why I didn't go screaming off for Mrs. Sullivan at once, but by the time I thought of doing it the screaming time had passed, and I hadn't let a peep out of me.

I got myself into the armchair and sat there thinking. '*I couldn't have. I couldn't have!*', and trying to convince myself that I *hadn't*.

I was scared to move out of the chair, in case something worse would happen, so I just sat there, and I must have gone to sleep eventually, because the next thing was . . .

"*Clare!*"

"C-L-A-R-E!"

There was a rattle of gravel against the window.

"Clare! The window, Clare!" Mo was trying to yell and whisper at the same time, so that Mrs. Sullivan wouldn't hear her.

Now I could tell Mo! That was my first thought. My second was: Tell her what? Tell her that I'd seen a spook in our room? She'd never let me live it down.

"Hurry up, Clare!" Mo moaned.

"Hurry up what?" I said, opening the window.

"I'm coming up the tree and you have to heave me in," Mo said.

That is just like Mo! I was in no fit condition for heaving anyone in. She made it under Mo-power.

"Crikey!" she said. "More damage!"

"Ripped your tights?" I said.

"Ripped me more like!" Mo said, sitting down on the floor and inspecting her leg, which was badly scraped from the tree climbing.

"What did you have the light on for?" she grumbled, getting to her feet.

I'd had the light on because I didn't fancy sitting in the room with it off, but I couldn't tell her that. If I told her I'd seen somebody in our room and then the somebody had disappeared she would laugh her leg off . . . not just the good one, both of them, scrapes and all. Then she'd start on about me making things up to get attention.

"Come in by the door, next time," I said.

She couldn't come in by the door, that was the whole point of it. She had to come in by the window; she wasn't supposed to be out late with her Mystery Man.

"I hope he was worth it," I said.

"Wouldn't you like to know?" she said.

She tossed her head, taking a look at herself in the mirror. She is nice looking, I suppose. *She* thinks she's gorgeous.

"I hope you had a good time," I said. "I've been *very* busy Maxie-minding."

Why couldn't I say what I wanted to? My mind was still all a-boggle. Here was my own sister, the one I should have been able to talk to if I was going to be able to talk to anyone, and I couldn't get the words out.

"Have you?" she said, as if she didn't know. Then she waltzed off on tiptoe to the bathroom to wash her leg, giving me the eyebrows as she went.

I sat there. I didn't move a muscle. I had to be going mad. Only mad people *see* people when there is nobody there.

She came back in, and floated round the room changing into her nightie and telling me how wonderful it was to feel grown up and how I would know what it felt like when it happened to me.

"Like mumps," I said. It didn't go down very well, and I could have bitten my tongue out when I said it. All I was doing was making it impossible to start talking about the one thing I wanted to talk about, which wasn't Mo's Mystery Man.

"Look," she said. "I'll look after Maxie tomorrow, will that do?"

"He's going out with the Archers in their boat," I said. "You know that."

"Then we don't have to worry about him, do we?" she said.

She got into her bed, and thumped her head down on the pillow. Then she thought about it, and re-arranged herself to look like the Lady of Shalott.

I lay in the darkness.

I didn't mind the light being off now that Mo was with me. It was the same old room we'd always stayed in at Garrison House, with the deep set window tucked in under the eaves and the wall clock that didn't work and the tiny fireplace. The room had a low ceiling and a crooked door. I should have put the mat against the door when Mo was out, to keep the light from shining across the hall, if I was going to have the light on. The Thought Police . . . adults everywhere . . . are sharp on things like that. Mo and I used to like sitting in the room in the dark, making toast on the one bar, but now Mo was having her adolescence, and I was left out.

"Mo?" I said.

"I don't think I'm talking to you any more, ever," she said.

"*Mo*," I said.

"Well?"

"Mo, did you ever see anything, anybody I mean, anybody who wasn't there?"

"No," she said.

"Ghosts," I said, finally getting round to it. "I was thinking how this house is three or four hundred years old and there could be ghosts in it, couldn't there? Ghosts of people who died here? There must have been people dying in this room, even."

"Oh, shut up," she said.

"Mustn't there?"

"I don't believe in spooks," she said.

"What about the Holy Ghost?"

"The Holy Ghost apart, I don't believe in spooks," Mo amended.

"Not at all?"

"No."

That was good. I didn't either.

I lay on for a while, wishing Mum was back. Then I turned over and went to sleep. I hadn't seen any Ghost Girl. I'd imagined her.

3

"Somebody was late out last night," said Mrs. Sullivan, giving me the beady eye. There was no one else to give it to. I was in the kitchen, helping her with the lunch dishes.

Mo was right! She'd warned me that the Thought Police were after us, and we'd spent most of the morning keeping out of Mrs. Sullivan's way.

"Your Daddy wouldn't like to hear about any goings on, my lady!"

Was she getting at me for taking Maxie out after his bedtime, or Mo for coming in through the window? I didn't know which. Maybe she thought I'd come in through the window, and Mo had been doing the Maxie-minding.

"We're allowed out late-ish on holiday," I said, selling my soul for loyalty, and not telling her it was Mo. Just the same I wanted to make my point. She wasn't Mum, she had no right to be Thought-Policing us around. I certainly wasn't going to have my life ruled by an Honorary Auntie in blue wellies. I don't know why she wears blue wellies, but she does most of the time.

It was Mo she should have been after anyway, not me. I hadn't *done* anything!

Yet!

I was going to, because I'd no intention of spending another evening Maxie-minding while Mo went out on the town. If it meant sitting in the shelter all evening, I was getting out of the house. Mo could take Maxie for walks and buy him ice creams. Mo could tell him stories.

"A pair of young girls like you shouldn't be running around the town at night on your own," Mrs. Sullivan said. "Not at your age. Some of the crew round here are young devils."

It didn't fizz on me. I nodded as if I was agreeing, and put away the dishcloth. You would think a guest house would have a dish-washer, wouldn't you? I'd have a dish-washer if it was me.

"I'll be having a talk with big sister later!" said Mrs. Sullivan, no doubt hoping that would put the fear of God in me. "But you mind what I say now!"

Mo was in for the Donegal version of the Birds and the Bees. I'd have to get her to tell me about it. Being Mo, she couldn't resist telling me in the end anyway. I get all that stuff from Mo, whether I want it or not.

She's not bad, Mo. She's my best friend, even if she is my sister, but being my sister gets in the way.

I made my excuses and went to look for the Canon. Maxie was off with the Archers, so I didn't have to worry about baby-minding.

Mrs. Sullivan had made an arrangement that I'd help the Canon sort out his things for the auctioneer. The Bishop was sending him back where he'd come from, Mayo or somewhere, and he was to leave the Church at Bonecastle, where he'd been for years. They were auctioning off the Parish House, and that is why he'd moved in with Mrs. Sullivan. It was a bit sad.

"They're leaving me to sink gently in the West," he said, as we went up Murray's Hill, and he bought me a bag of crisps when he was getting his *Catholic Herald* in the Gift Shop.

We reached the Parish House, and got started.

"I have my book to finish anyhow," he said, perched on the chair behind his desk.

"It isn't every Parish has a Hanged Priest, and a Rebel one to boot," he added, with a grin. "Mother Church tends to be conservative in her ways. *Father Maury, His Life and Times, and his Betrayal.*"

I smiled, politely. Everybody who came to Bonecastle heard about Father Maury, and had to go and look at the mouldy old memorial stone by the river. You'd think they could manage a proper statue! If it was me, I would expect a statue for being a Heroine of the Resistance! Hanged Priests are ten a penny in Ireland. With any other Catholic person I might have felt awkward about it, because *our* side did the hanging. My family (especially my Grannie Campbell) would have been selling flags for the British Legion, if there was a British Legion in 1744, and telling the soldiers to hang a few more National Heroes. I didn't feel awkward about it with the Canon, but on the other hand I didn't want to get involved in heavy conversations.

"Blood and thunder stuff!" the Canon said. "Right here on the doorstep. And with it I'll include my notes on the Parish, and its history, always making sure to include a page or two of the real hot gossip, which family paid for what, just to keep people happy. You'll like the adventure stuff. The Spy Priest and the soldiers . . . Mind you, I have doubts about the whole thing. There was no confession, did you know that?"

"Confession?" I said.

"I don't mean the Sacrament. I mean Maury never said a thing."

"Why would he, if they were going to hang him?"

"Oh well now, study your Patriotic Irish Heroes! They're great men for the speech from the scaffold. But Father Maury never said a word. The soldiers came up here and dragged him down the street to his death, and never a murmur out of him."

12

"Here? You mean this house?"

"No. But hereabouts. There was no Parochial House in Bonecastle till times improved. It would have been a cabin of sorts, the best the people could do. It was little enough they did for the man in the end, but watch him die with his lips sealed. He betrayed no man. And what thanks did he get from a man like Soraghan? I . . . but there you are! It is all over now. Father Maury is in his grave. He was either a terribly close man, or an innocent one."

"But he was hanged," I said, and immediately I felt embarrassed, because it sounded as if I was taking sides. Father Maury was a Catholic, and our side had hanged him. I sounded as if I was saying that we must have been right to do it.

"He was hanged in a hurry!" said Canon Roche. "It was 1744, and people were waiting for the French to come. Father Maury gave the authorities a chance to show the people the price they would have to pay if they picked the wrong side. Here now, wait until I show you this!" He pulled down a pile of old green journals from the shelves behind the desk, and selected the top one. "There. This is his. His journal for the year 1743."

The thin rusty letters spread across the pages of the old book, neat and sprawly at the same time.

"The man himself fingered that paper,"

Canon Roche announced. I think he felt I hadn't been much impressed up to then. He took the book from me, and carefully replaced it with the others. There were eight of them, each one marked with the year number on the back, from 1735 onward.

"It makes it *real*, doesn't it?" I said, touching the page.

"Real?" said the Canon.

"It is history . . . Father Maury is, but that journal is *real* and he wrote it, and here it is. It's a bit of history, it doesn't belong to *now*."

"You'd rather history stayed where it belongs?" said the Canon.

"Y-e-s," I said, uncertainly.

"This is where it belongs," he said. "This is where it happened."

We were all lined up for our tea when Maxie came in off the boat, with a fish.

"Did you catch it yourself?" Mo asked.

"Peter did," he said. "Peter gave it to me."

He was really delighted with himself. Mo had to take the fish and ask Mrs. Sullivan if she would cook it for him. I don't think Mrs. Sullivan was too pleased, but she cooked it anyway.

"You're the one who never eats fish," I told him, when he'd finished.

"It was brilliant," he said.

Mrs. Sullivan came in and took the dishes. I got up to help her, but she said: "No, dear, Maureen will give me a hand. Won't you, Maureen?"

Mo was already heading for the door, but that pulled her up sharp.

"Yes, Mrs. Sullivan," Mo said.

Mum said we had to help out because it wasn't just bed and breakfast, it was a friendly arrangement with Mrs. Sullivan as well.

I gave Mo a wink.

She was in for the Third Degree, over the dishes. I hoped she would have the wit to keep her mouth shut about coming in through the window, or I'd be in for it too.

I nipped up to our room to get my anorak.

Mo'd left our room in a bit of a mess.

She'd been doing something with the tongs.

They were in the fireplace, right up against the grate, and the red paper that was usually stuffed there was lying on the carpet, in shreds.

What was she tearing up red paper for?

If she was padding her bra I would have a good laugh at her! I thought she might be.

"You're padding your bra!" I said, when she came up.

"I am not!" Mo said.

"What were you tearing up the grate paper for then?" I said. "Tell me that!"

"Dirty old grate paper," said Mo in disgust.

"What do you pad it with then?" I said, quick as a flash.

"I've no need to pad my bra," said Mo. "I'm a good shape for somebody my age!"

She is. She was right.

"At least I *need* a bra," she added.

"I'm going out," I said, ignoring that one. What could I do but ignore it? "You can tidy up the mess."

I went for a walk out along the road, and then I walked back in again and down onto the beach. The Atlantic breakers were coming in and it should have been beautiful. The sound of the breakers mingled with the sound of Maguire's Fair . . . tinkle tinkle bonk bonk. It all made me feel lonely and I didn't want to speak to anybody.

I went up the steps, and over to the Fair.

"Big Game for tonight. Just about to commence. Come all ye, come all ye! Big Game about to commence this minute, in the saloon. A Big Game for Tip Top Prizes. Don't be shy! Come on in! We're all friends here! All Star Bingo!"

I crossed the fairground, untempted. Four ladies on stools sat against the Bingo counter. Fergie Reilly stood by the microphone in his shirtsleeves, looking at his gold wrist watch. In the daytime he runs one of the kiddy rides that

Maxie goes on. He gave me a wave. He's almost the only person I know in Bonecastle, outside the people at Garrison House.

I went down the street, past the Provo Shop. It's all full of Patrick Pearse and booklets about Irish Freedom and the Boys Behind the Wire. The way I was feeling then I'd have petrol bombed it, if I'd had a petrol bomb, just to get my own back. I went past it and I looked in, and the woman behind the counter was knitting a pair of baby's bootees.

How could she be doing that in there, when her lot were bombing us?

I went into a café and had a cup of coffee, though it was ruin on the finances. It was only half past nine.

I wasn't going home until after ten, so I could be sure I'd have to climb in the window, like Mo.

At twelve minutes past ten, I went up Murray's Hill.

Mo was watching from the window.

She knows I can't bear being watched.

She didn't want me to know that she was watching, so she kept back, but I could make out her figure standing there, looking at me.

I went for the gravel, to chuck at the window. Then she could put on the light and be surprised and say she'd just got out of bed, and she hadn't been up there watching me in the darkness.

"Clare!"

Oh dear! Oh help! It was Mrs. Sullivan. The Thought Police had got me.

"I was just closing up," she said, as I followed her into the hall, leaving a trail of gravel behind me as I tried to drop it without making any sound. Most of it had to go in my pocket.

"Did you have a good time, dear?" she asked, posing in front of her Personally Signed Photograph of Pope Paul Conveying His Blessing on Ignatius Sullivan and Mary Sullivan on the occasion of their Silver Wedding. It was very nice of the Pope to think of it. I don't understand why Catholics stick up things like that. With the picture, and the plastic Eternal Light Sacred Heart on the landing I felt like a foreigner . . . although the funny thing was I'd never felt that way before when we stayed there. I hadn't noticed how different it was. Grannie Campbell was right about that after all.

"I've had a brilliant time," I said, lying in my teeth.

I went to go upstairs.

"Your sister is in next door," Mrs. Sullivan said.

I stopped.

"With the Archer boys," she said. "Henry and Peter. *Their* TV is working!"

"Oh," I said.

"You could go in too," she said. "Mrs. Archer won't mind another in the crush."

"Yes," I said.

"Are you all right, Clare?" she said.

"Yes," I said.

"Sure?" she said.

"Yes," I said.

Then I went back out of the door, heading for the Archers, and I never once dared to glance up at the old dark window of our room in case I'd see *someone* in there, looking out at me.

It was *her*, up there, it had to be.

She'd come out of the wallpaper again.

4

I made up my mind to talk to the Canon about
it. He wasn't there at breakfast so I cleared off as
soon as I could to look for him.

He wasn't in the back garden of Garrison
House. He had hopped over the wall, and gone
up the hillside to the Castle. It isn't really a
Castle, just the crumbling remains of an old
bawn ... that's a fortified farmhouse ... no
more than twelve or fifteen metres high, haunted
by the Sullivans' goats. It's a great place for
slipping away to. A place to meet your Heathcliff
in, if you had one.

I hadn't got a Secret Lover, so I had to make
do with the Canon.

The Canon had his short legs stuck out in
front of him, and his bottom firmly set on a rock.
His dog collar was unhitched.

"I'm not myself," he said, when he saw me
coming. "I have a cold in the head. I'm sitting
here to let the wind blow it out of me."

"I wanted to ask you something, but you're
not to laugh at me," I said. "Is that all
right?"

"I'm promising nothing," he said.

"I've been worried. Could you answer me a question?"

Catholic Priests have got to believe in spooks and things, haven't they?

"I would, if I could, if you'd ask it," he said patiently.

"It's not a joke even if it sounds like a silly question," I said. "Only you are a clergyman even if you're . . . you're . . ."

"The Wrong Sort?" he said, gleefully. "Well now, your own man is up the hill with a fine black car to bring him down it. On the other hand, I have a bit of an advantage, d'you see? The Wrong Sort being the Right Religion helps a lot!"

He thought it was very funny.

I didn't.

Mr. Claremorris is the Church of Ireland Rector in Bonecastle. He is a drip. I couldn't ask him, and anyway I didn't want to. I wanted to ask the Canon because he is a nice *man*, no matter what religion he is.

I plunged in. "All I want to know is: Are there ghosts?"

"Yes," he said.

"Oh!"

"*Probably*, yes," he amended. "I'll say this to you. There may well be what you'd call ghosts. I don't know. According to the book there would have to be, wouldn't there? Well, that's good

21

enough for me. It is when you get to the headless horsemen and the visiting celebrities and that gang that I get worried."

"Yes?" I said. "You mean *yes*?"

"I've given you as straight an answer as I can, and not one I'd give everybody," he said. "You're an odd creature, with a brain that's bigger than your years, Clare. A plain answer. Now for a plain question. Why do you want to know?"

"I get a feeling sometimes that there's someone else in my room. Someone watching me," I added.

"You think there is someone around your room, like me with you here? Is that it? Only you can't see anybody? Well, maybe there is. How would I know? Maybe you're the next Bernadette . . ."

"Bernadette?"

"Saint Bernadette," he said.

"Me?" I said.

"I don't think so, either," he said. "But whatever you think is going on, it raises a big question. Why?"

"Why what?"

"You tell me. The answer to a question like that will likely lie inside you. If you think there's somebody watching you, what's there to watch?"

I felt myself flush.

"You'll tell me if you think any more about it, won't you?" he said.

I stood there. I didn't say anything.

"You're a bright child, Clare," he said. "Be careful of yourself, will you? And if you feel there's anything else you'd like to tell me, well, I'm available."

I nodded.

"Never mind about anybody else," he said. "We'll not tell them a dicky-bird."

He was trying to tell me that he was on my side, and he wasn't one of the Thought Police. I *half* believed him, but I still couldn't bring myself to tell him that I'd actually *seen* the Ghost Girl.

5

Graves Sunday.

"It's a local reunion," Mo said. "All the old island families collect together and go out to Big Tom once a year, to tend the graves. The Canon is going, and little Mr. Soraghan, and Mrs. Sullivan. She said we could go if we wanted to."

"I don't think I want to," I said.

"I think she'd like us to," said Mo. "She said we need pay no heed to the religious bit, but there would be nothing to prevent us going off round Big Tom by ourselves."

"Why does she want us to come?"

"I don't know," said Mo. "Mr. Sullivan was from the island, and now that he's dead she goes for him. Maybe having us there will help her some way, considering she has none of her own family to go with her."

Mrs. Sullivan's three children are all away.

"What about Maxie?" I said.

"All arranged," said Mo. "Maxie's going in with the Archers again. He plays with their Michael. Which is another good reason for going. If we get Maxie in as a fixture next door there won't be so much Maxie-minding to do, will there?"

That was the clincher! I'd reached the point where I'd do anything to get out of Maxie-minding, even if he was my own dear brother.

I went down to the Milk Harbour with Mo and Mrs. Sullivan and the Canon and Mr. Soraghan. There were a lot of people, and cars. They'd come in from their bungalows to clutter the steep and narrow road around the new Church of Our Lady of Grace. The wind blew the chip papers around the Sisters of Mary Grotto.

"Donegal must have been nice, once, when there were no people," I muttered to Mo. "No visitors in big cars, I mean. No bungalows."

"And all the local people starved and had to go off to America so they could send big cheques home to stop the starving," said Mo. "Big deal!"

We got into a boat with Mrs. Sullivan, Mr. Soraghan and Conor Brady. Conor let me steer. We set off for Little Tom, or Tomas Beg, as Mrs. Sullivan kept calling it, which was no more than a dark hump in the ocean, far beyond the end of the headland.

The rhythmic chug-chug of the boat's engine and the lap of the water around the bows formed a sleepy background to the day. Looking back at the town I could pick out the stump of the bawn above Garrison House, and the washing line which flapped up the hill where Mrs. Sullivan kept the goats. I thought I could make out a goat, but I wasn't sure.

"In the old days, when there was a trading fair at Bonecastle, the boats came from the island in fleets," said Mrs. Sullivan. "Fair day must have been a great event."

She'd left the wellies at home, the one day that she needed them. She had a blue suit on, and a white hat and a scarf, and blue court shoes.

"A big day," said Mr. Soraghan, who had perched in the stern in his best black suit and boots, with a scarlet handkerchief peeping out of the top pocket of his jacket. He was a brown wizened man, with small bones. He had a wispy moustache and thinning hair, which he wore carefully plastered along his head. I wondered if it was a top piece, but I couldn't ask Mo, in case he heard. It looked like hair he'd bought out of a Sunday paper, sight unseen.

"Your family is from the island, Mr. Soraghan?" Mo asked, politely. Too politely. I know Mo.

"We are," said Mr. Soraghan.

Mrs. Sullivan stirred, uneasily.

"Why are you not living on the island now?" Mo asked, in her innocent voice. I didn't know what was going on, but something was.

"There is no one on the island now," Conor Brady said, giving Mo a hard look.

26

Conversation died away.

Mo grinned at me. What was she grinning about?

We reached Tomas Beg, Little Tom, where a small group of islanders welcomed Mrs. Sullivan and Conor, and Mo and I got a formal introduction. Mr. Soraghan stayed in the boat, exchanging only the briefest of greetings with the Tomas Beg men.

It was half past twelve before we reached the mooring place at Tomas Mor. We were the last boat to land out of eight, all due to my brilliant steering! Mo and I followed the Sunday suits up the narrow track past the roofless houses to the stone walled burial ground, and the ruin of the tiny church.

There were more people than we had expected there to be.

Mr. Soraghan was apart from the rest, over by the wall on the far side, clearing away the weeds. Long grass grew in the tiny graveyard, and a few white trees bent against the crumbling wall.

"It feels *alive*, doesn't it?" Mo said, with her serious face on.

I knew what she meant. It wasn't plastic flowers in plastic cases, and white pebble graves. Just rough stone, and wild grass.

"Imagine leaving your houses to cows and goats," Mo said.

We'd been listening to the Tomas Beg men in

the boat. They still grazed cattle on the island, although no one lived there.

We got fed up watching the tidying, so we went on up the narrow track between the boulder walls that bordered the fields.

"It's like being on a different planet," Mo said. We had come out at the top, and we could see most of the island spread out around us. To the east, through the haze, we could make out the mainland, and the glistening of the sun on the caravans at Bailie's Strand, just outside Bonecastle. To the west the grey rocks led up to a formation called the Chimney, because it looked like one, and ended in a sheer drop through the rock bed to the sea. Mrs. Sullivan had made us promise to keep clear of the Chimney, in case we fell down it.

"Tomas Mor," I said. "The Island of the Betrayer!"

"Don't let Mr. Soraghan hear you say that," said Mo. "He mightn't appreciate it."

"Why . . . Oh!" Suddenly realisation dawned. I knew what the business on the boat had been all about!

"You're a fine one to talk!" I said. "No wonder Mrs. Sullivan was looking daggers at you!"

"What did I do?" said Mo, mock innocently.

"It's silly, anyway," I said. "Think about it! The *Soraghan* who betrayed Father Maury . . . that was 1744, just before the Jacobite Rising,

Bonnie Prince Charlie and Culloden and that lot! They couldn't still hold that against him, could they? I know Mr. Soraghan has the same name but . . ."

"Eoin Soraghan from Tomas Mor, the Betrayer. Oh yes they could!" Mo said, sitting down on a lump of stone like a dragon's egg. "If your Parish Priest was a Jacobite and one of his Parishioners betrayed him and then made off with the Parish silver plate, you'd remember him! Especially if the soldiers came and laid waste your homes afterwards, looking for him. That is why the Soraghans aren't exactly popular on Tomas Mor and Tomas Beg. If the originals hadn't gone to the mainland quickly, they'd have been chucked down the Chimney. I don't think the name Soraghan is too popular in Bonecastle either!"

"It wasn't silver plate," I said. "It was a golden crucifix, something Father Maury had brought from France. The Canon told me."

"I think that the Betrayer deserved all he got," said Mo, with relish. "I'm very pleased that the soldiers killed him in the end. Serve him right! I bet nobody missed him."

"1744 . . . that is more than two hundred years ago. It shouldn't matter to anybody now."

"What is two hundred years, out here?"

"Suppose he was *framed*," I said. "Wouldn't

29

that be awful? If he didn't do it. Imagine being called Betrayer if you weren't one."

"Stealing from a man who was being hanged, and a Patriot Priest at that, in Holy Ireland," Mo grinned at me. "He was lucky they didn't boil him in oil. I think it is very interesting the way they treat Mr. Soraghan, and the way he *expects* to be treated that way, but it doesn't stop him coming. It is to do with old primitive communities and things. We did a bit of that in school."

"TV and cars and central heating and fancy bungalows . . ." I said.

"It's a *feel* in the place," Mo said.

"Maybe we are all in a time slip," I said. "Maybe the red coats or the militia or whatever will come over the hill and we'll both get ravaged."

"Yummy!" said Mo.

"It wouldn't be one bit yummy," I said.

Mo stood up.

"They're gathering round the church," she said, looking back. "We'd better go down. It'll look odd if we're up here being ravaged when everyone else is being holy."

"Doesn't count for Protestants," I said.

"Come on," Mo said.

"I'm not taking orders from you," I said, but I went after her down the boulder wall path, because I didn't fancy being up there on my own.

"It is all in Latin," Mo whispered, when we were safely installed at the back of the crowd.

"It isn't supposed to be," I said. "The Pope said it had to be in native languages from now on."

"Well, that's Latin," said Mo. "Maybe what the Pope said hasn't got as far as Big Tom yet."

"If only Grannie Campbell could see us!" I said, and we both grinned.

Grannie Campbell would have gone mad if she'd known we were at a Catholic service. My dad says it isn't her fault, she just doesn't know any better. To hear Grannie Campbell you'd think all Catholics were in the I.R.A., and no Protestants ever laid finger on a bomb or gun.

We followed it as best we could. Canon Roche was impressive, and different from his usual wee bird self, although his cold was getting the better of him. He began to slur his words a little. I hoped we wouldn't be bringing him home in a box. The whole thing, the chanting and the beads and the Latin, made me feel awkward.

"I'm slipping off," I said, nudging Mo.

"Don't," Mo said. She was looking peaky. The wind was getting up, and it was blowing her hair round her.

I went away.

I had the oddest feeling, standing on the gateway step, listening to the muttered exchange of the priest and the people behind me. All those

31

people, answering as one when the Canon invoked them, voices from the now, mingling with voices from the *then*, those who had prayed before on the island, when the island was a community. All those voices seemed to well up against me, making me an intruder.

I went off quickly, down the track between the boulder walls, escaping from the voices and the Canon, and the past. I found myself in the middle of the clustered row of houses.

Doors and windows – so they were *houses*. Homes, cottages. Small cottages. *Very* small cottages. There were five of them, roofless, all leaning up against each other. They were so tiny that it was difficult to believe people had ever lived in them. Whole families had lived there. Work, sleep, breakfast, dinner and tea . . . if they'd had breakfast, dinner and tea . . . probably they hadn't. Probably it was work, sleep, starve. In the winter the gales ripped you apart, and in the time of Father Maury's Betrayal and the '45 the soldiers came and burned your places round you. Whole families, in those tiny hovels.

It was all gone now. Mrs. Sullivan had told me there was no one left who had lived on Tomas Mor, and only eight families on Tomas Beg.

I went into one of the houses. Darkened stone, where the hearth had been. Earthen floor, where nettles and thistles grew . . . and four Coke tins, wrapped in a plastic bag.

I closed my eyes, just to feel what it might have been like, when the place had a roof, and a fire, and people, but I couldn't feel it at all.

I went out and sat on a stone in the sunlight. I had no place on Tomas Mor.

Mo scarpered off upstairs when we got home, but I went into the Guest Lounge and made small talk with Mr. Soraghan, for the good of my soul! Mo shouldn't have been stirring it, and I wanted to make it up to him.

I was on my way upstairs when the kitchen door opened and Mrs. Sullivan signalled out of it, for me to come down to her.

"What now?" I thought, but I went.

"You two girls were at the Mass on the island?" she said.

"We didn't mean any harm," I said. Perhaps she thought it was rude, or interfering. "We didn't think anyone would mind. We don't know what your services are like. We . . ."

"Nobody minds, child," said Mrs. Sullivan, cutting me short. "Nobody minds that at all. But just a word in your ear, in case you might hear talk."

"Talk?"

"Canon Roche," she said. "It was a big day there for him, d'you understand? The last time he'll go there. And what no one knows, no one will make any trouble about, isn't that so?"

"Trouble?" I said, and then I got it. "You mean the Latin? He shouldn't have been saying Mass in Latin, should he?"

"There now!" said Mrs. Sullivan, looking surprised. "You're a bright girl, you are. How did you know that?"

"I read it somewhere."

"Books are great!" she said, as though they were some new invention. I felt like asking her why she hadn't got any, apart from *Old Moore's Almanac, 1948.*

"In a newspaper," I said.

"Is that so?" she said. "Well, there we are! The Canon is too old to change his ways. But it wouldn't do if some of the new people here got to know about it, d'you see? It is all right when it is just the islanders. But we do not want Him in His Bungalow to hear tell."

Who *was* Him in His Bungalow? I hadn't an earthly, but as I didn't know him I wasn't likely to tell Him!

"There would be a Holy fuss if it ever got about," said Mrs. Sullivan. "Mum's the word!"

She gave me a chocolate biscuit, shaped like a Teddy Bear.

I went up the stairs, nibbling it.

"Look at this mess!" said Mo.

The crêpe paper which we'd put back in the fireplace was all over the floor. The hearth mat lay in a ball against the leg of the chair. The shovel and tongs were up-ended in the grate, and there were marks like scratches on the sooty bricks at the back of the fire-basket.

"Is this one of your silly jokes?" Mo asked.

"No," I said.

"Maxie?" Mo said.

"Maxie's been next door all day," I said.

"Okay," said Mo. "*Who-dunnit?*"

She didn't know the answer, and neither did I.

6

We were asleep, but I woke up ... it would
be me!

The girl was there again, but this time she
was standing at the foot of my bed, looking down
at me.

She had long black hair that framed her pale
face.

She looked at me steadily, not smiling. She
didn't move. It was as if she couldn't manage the
effort.

Her hands were folded in front of her. I could
see the blue veins in them. I could see her dainty
fingernails. She had a little ring, a child's thing,
on her left hand.

I didn't move.

She didn't move.

I don't know how long it lasted.

Afterwards, I lay in the darkness. I didn't
wake Mo. I wouldn't have known what to say to
her and, anyway, I wasn't afraid.

'*It's this room*,' I thought. '*She's part of this room.*'

I closed my eyes, and I could feel the room
about me. I'd touched it in some way, and its
past was oozing out of the crooked walls, right

through the rose and petal wallpaper and the religious pictures and the plastic flowerpots on the mantelpiece.

I had said or done or felt something that had released the past, and the girl had come to me.

7

"What did this apparition look like?" Canon Roche said, putting down his paper. He was out at the bawn, recovering after the effort of eating his breakfast.

"Pale. A bit bigger than me. Not very well."

"She'd be dead, of course, you're assuming that?" said the Canon. "That would account for not looking well."

Was he pulling my leg? I couldn't be sure. Perhaps it was the way he had of making everything sound like the beginning of a joke that he never quite got round to finishing.

"She was like you and me," I said.

There was a long pause, while he folded his paper, and put it in his pocket.

"Continue," he said. "I want to know what you *think* happened. You have my interest. It's only a way of talking I have."

"She didn't look well," I said. "Sort of drawn, and tired. She had long black hair, and a grey dress with white cuffs, and saddish eyes."

"What are saddish eyes?"

"Well, as if she had been crying ten minutes before, but wasn't any more. You know?"

"I see."

"She was very pretty. Well, *no*, she wasn't. She was beautiful in a sad way. Not a Beauty Queen with legs and things. She was clean, and neat, with wee lace cuffs, and her hair was shiny and long, right down her back."

"Did you *see* that?" he said.

He thought he'd caught me out. I'd told him she didn't move, and she was facing me.

"I saw her hair the first time," I said.

"The first time?"

"I saw her once before," I said. "I didn't tell anybody."

"It is a remarkable story," said the Canon. "I don't know that I've heard the like. You wouldn't pull an old man's leg, would you?"

"I'm not making it up," I said.

"I hope you're not," he said.

"In a way I wish I was. Because no one will believe me. But I *did* see her, and then there's the thing about the crêpe paper, and the fireplace."

"That might be a draught of some kind."

"It wasn't. The tongs were moved about, and so was the mat. Draughts don't do that. And what about the marks on the back of the fireplace?"

"Mice?"

"Mrs. Sullivan wouldn't have mice. Bord Failte would strike her off the Tourist List."

"Mice can happen to anyone. Especially in an

39

old house. This is a very old house. It used to be a garrison for the English. There's been a lot of building up and pulling down since that time. Lots of nooks and crannies. Three or four hundred years of them, if you went back to the original structure."

"It is not mice. It is something in my room," I said. Why wouldn't he talk seriously?

"Like big sister?" he said.

"Mo wouldn't play tricks on me," I said. "Well, she would. But not tricks like that." I don't think the Canon is all that keen on Mo.

"I'll tell you what I'll do," he said. "I'll go up and have a look for myself, if I may?"

We went up to the room.

Mo's tights were on the chair, in a ball. I stuffed them under the cushion.

The morning sun was streaming into the room. The crêpe paper was back in the fireplace. The brush and the poker and tongs hung on their hooks on the fire-stand.

"If you move the crêpe paper, you can see the marks," I told him.

The Canon bent down, and pulled the paper aside.

"There," I said, pointing to the scratches on the fire-bricks.

"Well, you could call them marks, I suppose," said the Canon. "But if the wind moved the crêpe paper, it would scrape the back . . . like that." And he demonstrated. "If there had been more soot, we would have been able to tell better, but our landlady keeps a neat house."

"You don't believe me?"

The Canon climbed up off his knees, replacing the crêpe paper as he did so. He banged his hands against the sides of his thighs, and looked at me.

"I believe you," he said. "I believe something or other out of the way has happened to you, and I believe you are doing your best to describe it. But that's all! To begin with, you told me you thought somebody was watching you. The last man who told me that was carted off in a big white van for calling himself St. Patrick. All right, don't jump down my throat. If there is *something* here, I would have a plain duty to help. But it is not a thing I could take on lightly. I doubt if our man in his bungalow would be pleased!"

"Who?" I said. People kept on about the man in the bungalow.

"Father Terence," he said. "My replacement here. He is the man in charge now. He might take the view that exorcism would not go down well with the Parishioners, or with Mrs. Sullivan. We would end up in the Sunday papers. I'm a bit long in the tooth for that."

"Couldn't you do it kind of quietly, never let on? Like you did on the island, with the Latin?"

He stiffened. I'd hit a weak spot.

"I don't think so," he said. "I don't think so, child."

"Why not?" I said.

"It would become a political thing, d'you see? Church politics! There is such a thing as Church discipline, though you might not believe it. I have no authority here now, none at all. Anything of that sort will be up to the new man."

"And you don't think he would do it?"

"He has his hands full with Cormac Crilly and the St. Vincent de Paul and getting new carpets for his bungalow. Then there's the Auction, and the sale of the Parish House. I wouldn't wish the man more trouble."

"But what about *her* . . . *it* . . . my apparition, if that is what you call her?"

"I say we sit tight, and see what happens next," said the Canon.

I think he was relieved to get away from me. It wasn't a satisfactory answer, in fact it was no answer at all.

I stayed in the room, after he'd gone downstairs.

It wasn't my fault.

I never asked to get landed with it.

I wished my Mum and Dad were back. There were plenty of people around, but I was lonely. That was what had been wrong with the holiday right from the start. I'd come away thinking I'd have Mo to talk to, but Mo wasn't interested in me any more. It was bad enough being lonely when there was nothing happening, but now I had a real problem, and there was no one to turn to. The ones I had thought would help had let me down.

I went down to the Guest Lounge, and played a game of Snap with Maxie.

8

'AUCTION TODAY' said the big sign by the roadside, and the cars were parked in a jumble around it.

"You don't *have* to come," I said to Mo.

"I think I will," she said. She didn't sound enthusiastic about it.

I was surprised. I hadn't been honoured with big sister's company much, and all of a sudden she was holding-my-hand . . . in a manner of speaking that is.

"I've never been to an Auction," Mo said, too brightly, as if going to an Auction was a big, exciting treat life had been keeping from her.

Neither had I, but I wasn't fussed about it. I wouldn't have been going, but I had a special commission for the Canon.

"It would never do for me to bid myself," he'd explained to me. "It wouldn't be right and proper. If I bid myself at the Parish House Auction, the people will stand back, you can rely on Cormac Crilly for that. And that is not right. The Auction is for Parish Funds, and for Father Terence's new bungalow. Everything must find its right price. I will put in my bid with the rest."

44

"But you can't," I said. "You've just said that."

"I will send an agent," he said. "Someone no one will think of. And who better than yourself? Unless you are shy of bidding?"

"Oh no. I'm not. Only how do you bid?"

"You just shout out how much you will pay," said the Canon. "That is all there is to it. Loud and clear now, so that Cormac can hear you!"

So I was deputised Auction-bidder for the afternoon!

"What are you supposed to be bidding for?" Mo asked me, as we pushed through the crowd in the study.

"The old clock on the mantel. The one with the brass face."

"139," said Mo, reading the lot number. All the things in the Auction had little tickets on them, with a number.

"We'll stay near it, to see if anybody else looks at it," I said. "The Canon says it is not going, so maybe nobody else will want it."

A lot of people looked at the clock.

I couldn't tell whether they wanted it or not. We stayed where we were, and Mo said things like: "I hear that old clock is no good," in a loud voice, when anyone seemed particularly interested.

"That's not fair," I told her. "The Canon said it was to get its right price, and he would bid

45

higher, provided it was no more than fifty pounds."

"It's not my fault if people listen in to conversations!" said Mo. "I'm not telling *them* that the clock doesn't work. I'm telling *you*. If they *insist* on overhearing, that is their hard cheese."

The Auction started in the hall, with lots of old carpet, and some stair rods, and some bedding.

"Who will open me at £10? A fine square this, just a touch of wear."

"It's *threadbare*!" I whispered.

"£5. £5 only. No extra charge for the dust!"

"Why is nobody bidding?" I whispered.

"Nobody wants it, stupid," said Mo.

"£4 then. Who will start me at £4? Come on. Must be sold, gentlemen. Ladies, a fine square. £3.50. Who will start me at £3.50? No? £3? £2? At £1 then?"

"50p," said a lady, at the front, with what looked like a tea cosy on her head.

"50p! 50p I am bid. £1. £1.50 on the left. £2. £2.50. £3. £3.50 I am bid. £4. Is that a bid? £4.50 on my right. It's against you, Madam. £4.50 on my right. £5! £5 on my left. I am bid £5. The lady's bid. £5 it is. Any more? Going at £5? £5.50. £6. Any more? A fine square. £6. Going at £6. At £6. At £6 . . . Gone! Mrs. Croskery, isn't it? A fine square!"

The lady with the tea cosy on her head pursed her lips in triumph.

"I don't *see* anybody bidding," I said.

"People just nod," Mo said.

It was most confusing. The Canon was wrong. They didn't shout out what they were going to pay. They let Mr. Crilly the Auctioneer go low down in price, and then they started bidding.

"I'll bid for you, if you like?" Mo said.

"I'll do it myself," I said. It was my special commission.

"All right, then," said Mo, flouncing her hair. She thinks she's good looking when she does that.

"£32 then? Any increase? Going at £32! Gone. The lady in the yellow hat. Bidding for Mr. Aidan Rice. Is that right? Lot 7, Mr. Rice, £32. Got that, Fergie?"

Fergie Reilly from the Bingo Saloon at Maguire's Fair was taking down the names on a big pad he had.

"Now the dresser. Wormed, it says here. No extra for the worm, not today."

"I wouldn't mind being an Auctioneer," I said, but I was talking to nobody. Mo had wandered off.

I sat down by the clock and waited. There were a lot of people, and they all seemed to know what they were doing. Maybe I should have let

Mo do the bidding for me, because she is bigger, and I might disappear altogether if somebody came and stood in front of me. It would have been easier to let Mo bid for me, and less embarrassing, but I wasn't going to give her the satisfaction. I wished I hadn't got into it, all the same. The Canon's money was burning a hole in my pocket, and I had to take it out every three minutes to see that it was still there.

Mr. Crilly talked very fast, and Fergie kept tearing off sheets and sending them through to the back scullery, where Mr. Crilly's clerk made out the bills.

". . . £14. £14 I am bid. £15. £16. Will anybody raise £16? £16 for Mrs. Archer. £17. £18. £19 on my right. Who will raise me £19? Do I see £20? No? Going at £19 then. Going. Gone! Lot 23, Mrs. Archer."

Mrs. Archer didn't look very pleased.

If Mrs. Archer was at the Auction, who was looking after Maxie, and her Michael?

The bidding took ages. Interesting things, like an old scrapbook of the Austrian Alps with some Nuns on skis, went for a few pounds, while some mouldy things fetched a fortune. I couldn't help wondering where the Canon was, and what he felt like, seeing the things he had lived with being divided up, ready to be carted off by strangers from the bungalows.

"Mrs. Clarke?" said the Auctioneer. "Is that

your bid? Hold on a minute! Mr. Clarke is bidding against you!"

There was a roar of laughter, and Mrs. Clarke slumped down on the Canon's sofa, red in the face. I didn't think it was all that funny, but everybody else did.

"I've broken many a good home that way," beamed the Auctioneer. "Now. The bidding is with *Mr.* Clarke, at a fiver. £6? No. At a fiver, then, Mr. Clarke. Can I tempt your good lady to bid against you? No? Sold to Mr. *and* Mrs. Clarke, at £5."

It went on and on.

"Who will open me £15? Is that right? I have £15 at the back. £20. £25. £30. £40. £50. £60. £75. £80. £90. £100. £105. £106. £107. £108. £108.50. No fifties. £109. £110. £115 . . . that's more like it now! £115 at the back. £120. More? At £120 . . . gone! Lot 138, Mr. Gawn. Lot 139, fine old mantel clock, brass face. Who'll start me at £60? £50 then? £40. I have £40. £45. £50. £60. £75. £80. £90. £95. £100. £110. £120. £130. £140. Enough, sir? £140. The bidding's with you, sir. £140, with the gentleman on my right. £140? Going at £140. . . . Gone!"

"That was *you*!" Mo hissed. "You didn't bid. You didn't open your mouth."

"Bannon, Ballyshannon," said the Auctioneer, and Fergie wrote it down on his pad.

"I *did* bid," I said. "I don't think he heard

me in the rush. £140! I wouldn't have got it anyway."

"You're *useless*," said Mo, unfairly.

I bit my lip, and then I wished I hadn't, because I bit it so hard it hurt. Bannon, Ballyshannon, had the Canon's old clock, which he'd wanted to take with him to Mayo. It wasn't my fault, but it was very disappointing. Some stranger from Ballyshannon, walking off with the old man's clock, the clock that had been on his mantelpiece for years.

"I bet there's a digital clock in the bungalow," I muttered.

"What bungalow?" asked Mo.

I didn't tell her.

"We can go home now, can't we?" said Mo.

"You go," I said. "I might want to bid for something."

I was going to show her I could bid, just like anybody else.

I bid for a work basket, and didn't get it.

"Are you not gone yet?" I said to Mo.

Then she bid for a hassock, and got it for 50p.

"What do you want that for?" I asked.

I knew fine well what she wanted it for. She wanted it to go one up on me.

"Sitting on," Mo said. "I shall sit and dream dreams."

"Oh *help*!" I said. "What about?"

"None of your business," she said.

The Auction moved upstairs, and I trooped up after everyone else. I was going to bid for *something*, that was certain sure.

"Lot 230. Box of oddments. What am I bid? Who will start me at £3. £2 then? £1? 50p?"

"25p!" I said, as loud as I could.

"25p. 25p to the young lady. 30p. 30p at the back. Against you?"

He looked at me, and winked.

"40p," I said.

"45p."

"50p," I said. I wasn't risking nods.

"50p I am bid. It's against you at the back 50p to the young lady. Going at 50p. Gone! Name, Miss?"

"Campbell," I said "My name's Clare Campbell."

"Campbell," he said, ignoring the Clare bit. I shouldn't have said the Clare bit. They were all looking at me standing there on my famous feet.

"Is that the same as the other Campbell, Cormac?" asked Fergie. You would think he would have known me. He always waves at me. Maybe he waves at everybody.

"No, different," I said.

"Campbell, Number Two," said the Auctioneer. "Put Campbell Number Two in your book."

"Campbell Number Two," said Fergie.

"You're Number One, and I'm Number Two," I said, when Mo poked her head into the second bedroom.

"Hi, Number Two!" said Mo.

She was being all cheerful again.

"I thought you'd gone home," I said.

"I thought I'd stay until you were finished," she said.

I didn't say anything for a minute.

"You didn't want to come," I said. "Who made you?"

"Nobody," she said, too quickly.

"The Canon?" I said. "Was it the Canon?"

"Okay," she said. "Okay, it was the Canon. He got on at me about leaving you on your own too much. He said you needed company. So I said I'd come."

"That was big of you," I said.

She'd gone over to the Thought Police on me!

"I might have come anyway," said Mo, tagging along behind me as we went to the last room.

She was trying to make out that she hadn't been tipped off that I was going potty and needed somebody to hold my hand. I wasn't having any. I was just mad with her, and the Canon.

"Another box of oddments. Lot 235. What have we here? Pictures. Three forks, plated.

Cigarette case. Who will say £3? £2 I am bid. At £2? Going. Gone!"

The crowd had thinned out, considerably.

"236. A locket, with a miniature portrait. That should have been down below, Fergie. Should have been. Still . . . an old locket, gentlemen . . . and ladies!" He gave a bow in our direction. "Who will bid for this? Come along . . . a piece that belonged downstairs in the cabinet, I'd say. But never mind. Who will bid me £10? £8 then? £5? Who will start me at £5? Mr. Bannon? £5 for Mr. Bannon."

"£5.*50*," I said.

I didn't even look to see what he was like. He had the Canon's clock, and that would do him.

"£6. It's against you, Miss. Who will raise me? It shouldn't be sold at £6. I have no authority to withdraw. Mr. Bannon's bid . . . will nobody raise me?"

"£6.50," I said, despite Mo tugging at me.

"£6.50 I am bid. £7? £7 I am bid . . ."

"£7.50," I said.

"At £7.50. The bid is against you, sir? At £7.50. Locket with miniature. Any more now? Any more before we go home for our tea? At £7.50. Going to the young lady at £7.50. At £7.50. Going. Gone! Sold to Miss Campbell."

"Is that Campbell One or Two, Cormac?" asked Fergie.

"You're absolutely batty!" said Mo, when she got me out of the room.

"I wasn't going to let him have it," I said. "He got the Canon's clock."

"£7.50!" she said. "Have you *got* £7.50?"

"Just about," I said.

"You never even looked at it. You don't know whether it's any good or not. £7.50!"

"It's a locket and picture," I said. "It's bound to be worth £7.50."

"Is it?" said Mo. "That man Bannon is a dealer. If he reckoned he could get money for it, he would have bought it."

"I'll have to use some of the Canon's money," I said, because I didn't want to hear any more. "I have just about enough at home to cover it, I think. Unless . . . maybe I could ask them to wait?"

"Cash with sale," said Mo. "That's in the Conditions of Sale in the hall. Didn't you read them?"

I shook my head.

"You are a fearful baby, Clare, sometimes," Mo said. "Why did you do it?"

"I wanted it," I said.

We went to the back scullery to pay our bills.

"Campbell One," said Mo, shoving forward as usual. "Lot 184, 50p."

But it wasn't 50p. It was 50p plus commission.

"I don't think that's fair," said Mo.

The commission didn't make much difference on the 50p, but it ruined me!

"50p, lot 230. What was the other one? Lot 235? £7.50. That makes £8. £8 at 8% commission. £8.64. And VAT."

"I'm bust," I said, as we went to collect our stuff. Mo got her hassock, and then I showed the receipt for the box of oddments, and then we went into the last room, where I'd beaten Bannon from Ballyshannon, and bust myself in the process.

I handed over my receipt, and the man gave me the locket and chain.

I opened the locket.

It wasn't really unexpected. All the way up the stairs from the scullery the feeling had been growing on me and now, before I opened it, I *knew*.

Her eyes were smiling, and she had her hair up. She was wearing an off-the-shoulder gown, like an old-fashioned evening gown, but there was no doubt about it.

The face in the locket, looking up at me, was the face of the Ghost Girl.

9

"Is that so?" said the Canon, looking down at the locket, which nestled in the palm of his hand. The tiny face gazed up at him.

"Well now," he said. "There is a difficulty here, and I'm duty bound to point it out to you."

"What?"

"You see . . . you described the girl you had seen. She had long black hair, round her, and tired eyes. A *drawn* face, you said. This girl, the girl in the picture here . . . she has fine features, all right, but you couldn't call them drawn. And she's rosy cheeked, a bit of a bright spark, I'd say, like your big sister! And there's no grey dress and cuffs, is there? This is a young madam on the make, and no mistake!"

I took the locket back from him.

"It *is* her," I said.

The Canon gave a shrug. We were all alone in what was left of his study. Mo had skipped off after the Auction. He was looking tired, and a bit sorry for himself, but I wasn't going to let him off with saying I was wrong.

"It's her, looking cheerful and all done up to have her picture taken. Painted, that is. And maybe the artist painted her rosy cheeked, when she wasn't. Or maybe this was a different time. Maybe she'd been ill when I saw her. After all, we know she's dead, don't we? And if she's dead she must have died of something, mustn't she? I expect she was ill. I expect she was ill in *my* room, and feeling lonely like I was, wishing she could be out with her friends and . . . and things like that. It could be that, anyway," I finished lamely, because I didn't think I was getting through to him.

"Who knows?" said the Canon. "Maybe. Maybe not." He took the locket from me again. The clip was bust. It didn't look much. It wasn't even very well painted.

"I wonder where it came from?" he said. "It is not a thing I've seen before. No doubt Father Tom could tell us."

"Let's ask him," I said.

"He's a long time in a better place," said the Canon.

"Couldn't we go and see him?"

"Not yet a while," said the Canon. "He's with them upstairs!" He raised his eyes to the heavens.

"Oh," I said, feeling stupid.

"Father Tom used to be Parish Priest here. I daresay this dates back to his time . . . or before it, to judge by her ladyship's dress. There was a lot of old stuff at the top of the house. So many curates, you see, when they had to cover the islands, before the people left. Now there is no need. The Parish house is too big a barn. Your man in the bungalow will toot around in his mini and cover the ground four men did before him."

The Canon was back on home ground again, grousing about the new man and the bungalow.

"I'm sorry about the clock," I said, taking the locket from him, and slipping it into the pocket of my anorak. "And about the money. I'll pay you back what I owe you, as soon as Mum and Dad get back."

"Don't mind that," he said.

He was standing in the middle of the study, which was a study no more. The bare boards beneath his feet creaked, and the green velvet curtains on the window hung awaiting a claimant, still tagged with their lot number. In the fireplace stood the gilt mirror, which someone had taken down from over the mantel, making a mess of the plaster when they undid the screws. I could see the Canon's knees reflected in it, cut off from the top of his body. They looked lonely.

"I can see your knees," I said. "In the mirror. Look."

He didn't look. I don't think he heard me. He was back in another time, with a carpet on the floor, and his clock on the mantelpiece, ticking. I'm sure he didn't even know I was there, or if he did I was playing the part of some long dead parishioner.

"*Canon?*" I said.

He gave a sigh. "We'd better hurry back, or we'll miss our tea," he said.

We went out of the back door into the hall, passing Bannon from Ballyshannon's men, who were removing the Canon's old mahogany sideboard. The Canon flicked his hat from the hallstand, placed it firmly on his head, and walked out through the front door, without shutting it.

"Not a bad toss, Canon!" Fergie Reilly called out.

"A brave day, Fergie. A brave day!" said the Canon.

I followed him down the street, toward Garrison House. It was cold, and the wind whipped our faces.

He never said a word the whole way.

10

The Canon took his tea in his room, and didn't come downstairs afterwards.

"He's tired, child," said Mrs. Sullivan. "The Auction took it out of him."

"I didn't see him. Not until after it was over."

"I daresay you wouldn't. That's his way. But let him be, now. He is an old man. It can't be easy to leave a place you've lived in for thirty years and see it sold up around you."

"I suppose not," I said.

Mo did her disappearing act after tea, and I put on my anorak and took Maxie out, because I was feeling guilty about neglecting him, and I wanted some company.

We went down by the Hanged Priest to the shore, and Maxie spurted off.

I sat down on a rock, and took the locket out of my pocket.

It *was* her.

The eyes were the same.

Why would nobody believe me?

Nobody was just the Canon, really. I hadn't asked anybody else.

"Ambush!" yelled Maxie. "G-E-R-O-N-I-M-O!"

"Bang, bang," I said. "You're dead. I spotted you by the hat."

I'd made him put on his hat, the one with Maxie on it, even though he didn't want to. There was a real wind blowing, and I didn't want to get into trouble for freezing Maxie.

He went off to plan another ambush.

"Hi there!"

It was Peter Archer, Maxie's friend. The one who got Maxie the fish. He's a year older than me, and two years younger than Mo. He isn't bad.

"Hallo," I said.

"Having a walk?" he said, and he came slithering down the rocks from the promenade, and ended up beside me.

"Walking Maxie," I said.

"I was beginning to think that that was my job," Peter said, with a grin.

I looked at him.

"Did Mrs. Sullivan ask you to do it?" I asked.

"Mrs. Sullivan asked my Ma, and my Ma *told* me," Peter said.

"The Thought Police again!" I said, and then I had to explain to him what that meant.

"I wish people wouldn't bother," I said.

"Why?" he said. "Why shouldn't people bother?"

"Because Maxie's my business. And how I feel

is my business. If I'm fed up walking Maxie, that's my business too."

We mooched along. Maxie ambushed us, and Peter chased him, caught him, and made-believe he was going to chuck Maxie into the sea, but he didn't.

We came up by the steps.

Mr. Soraghan was standing on the strand, looking out to sea. He looked lonely.

"I'm sorry for him," I said.

"There you are, you see," he said. "Now you're doing it."

"But I'm not interfering," I said.

"You would if you could, wouldn't you?" he said. "Anybody would."

"Well, okay. I would."

"That's not Thought Police," he said.

Mr. Soraghan got into his car and drove off along the Ballyshannon Road.

We took Maxie into the Fair, and Peter stood him a go on the roundabout. I couldn't stand anybody anything, because I had no money.

"That was great!" said Maxie.

"You ought to thank Peter, Maxie," I said.

"Thank you, Peter," Maxie said.

"It's my pleasure," said Peter.

He walked us home, up the street.

It was better than that, really. He walked *me* home, despite my big feet.

Maxie was just an ambushing-extra.

I put Maxie to bed, and then I went down-stairs, to see what was on TV. As usual, there was nothing but a buzz. If I had a guest house the TV would *work*.

"Just in time!" Mrs. Sullivan said, and she brought me into the kitchen for a cup of tea.

I told her all about the Auction, and she talked on about the Canon . . . it was funny the way even Mrs. Sullivan never talked about Mr. Soraghan. It was as if he had never been in the house at all.

I showed her the locket.

"Where'd you get this?" she asked.

"It's the one I got at the Auction. The one I told you about."

She looked at it for a long time. Then she said "Very nice!" and handed it back to me.

She had a funny look on her face.

"You don't know who it is, d'you?" I said.

"How would I?" she said, and then she got up and became very busy sorting out her knitting patterns.

Mo came in, on the dot of ten, saving us all from a row. Mrs. Sullivan put on the kettle and we had another cup of tea and talked about my Mum and Dad, and then Mo went off upstairs.

"Lipstick!" said Mrs. Sullivan, winking at me.

"What?"

"Big sister! She was licking at the lips, so I wouldn't see it!"

"Oh," I said. Mo had fooled me. I'd never have noticed.

"I thought lipstick was out, nowadays," said Mrs. Sullivan.

"It *depends*," I said. I was going to make sure Mo gave me a go with it. Mum doesn't use it, and I wanted to know what it felt like. Mo'd only say I was too young, and give me her I'm-Grown-Up bit.

"I'm for bed," Mrs. Sullivan said. She was in the hall, and I was on the stairs, when she called up to me.

"Did you enjoy yourselves, dear?" she asked.

I didn't catch on what she meant.

I settled for a nod.

"Young Peter's a nice lad," she said.

I went up to our room.

"What's the matter with you?" Mo said. "You're blushing scarlet!"

"Lipstick!" I said, going on the attack.

"Did *she* spot it?" asked Mo, anxiously.

"Didn't she just!"

"Oh . . . *heck*!" said Mo.

"Don't worry," I said. "She'll not tell."

"I don't care if she does tell," said Mo. "I'm not a child."

I grinned.

"Mum and Dad won't mind, anyway," she said. "Will they?"

"Not a bit," I said. "Out till all hours,

climbing in through windows, and now you are a painted lady!"

"Shut up!" Mo said, and went out to the bathroom.

I flopped down on the bed, then I propped myself up on my elbows and took out the locket. I stuck it on the bedside table, open, so I could look at her.

Then . . . *click!*

It more or less fell apart. There was a hidden hinge at the back, and it had bust. The picture fell forward on to the glass. There was something in the back.

Hair. A tiny lock of dark hair, in a twist of paper, stuck on the back of the picture. It wasn't glued, just pressed so long in position that it stayed there. It came away as soon as I touched it.

The hair was soft, and silky, and really creepy to touch.

Was it *her* hair, or somebody else's?

I rolled back the small bit of paper, which had been twisted round it. The paper was old, but the writing was delicate, and neat.

LUCIE SORAGHAN

11

CRASH!

"Wha . . .!"

We were both awake, shocked by the sound reverberating round the room. I hunched myself up in the bed and thrust out a hand for my lamp, just as Mo's went on.

Mo was wide-eyed with sleep.

"What on earth?" she said, blinking.

It was cold, very cold, colder than ordinary night-time cold. The clock was showing a quarter past three.

The fire-basket was lying side-on in the grate, as if someone had thrown it down there. One leg had snapped off. The crêpe paper lay in a crumpled ball at one side of the hearth, but the fire-bricks had been placed neatly, on top of each other, to one side.

"Did you do that?" Mo demanded.

"No," I said, sounding shaky, because I was.

She was out of bed and straight over to me.

"Are you all right, Clare?"

"Yes," I said.

There was a loud knock at the door, and then it opened, and Mrs. Sullivan danced in. She had her hair up in curler things and she looked like something out of Dr. Who.

"What was the racket? Did you have an accident, or something?"

"I . . . I don't know, Mrs. Sullivan," said Mo, standing up. "Clare's all right."

"The mess!" exclaimed Mrs. Sullivan, spotting it.

"We didn't do it!" said Mo, quickly.

I didn't say a thing. I lay where I was. Mo could do the talking.

"The crashing wakened us up and we put on the light, and it was just like that. We didn't do it, honestly, Mrs. Sullivan," Mo said, going red.

It didn't sound convincing.

"Would you look at that!" exclaimed Mrs. Sullivan. "The basket is broken up . . . and the leg of her is right through the back of the fireplace."

She picked up the fire-basket, joggling it free from the back of the fireplace, where there was a hole about the size of a ten pence piece.

"We didn't do it. Honestly we didn't." Mo said, getting desperate.

"If you didn't, who did?" Mrs. Sullivan said, sharply.

"I don't know," said Mo.

"Clare?" said Mrs. Sullivan.

"I didn't," I said. "*Honestly*."

There was a long silence, while she stood

looking at us. Then she bent down and started picking things up.

"Is it burglars, trying to make off with the tongs?" she said, dryly.

I opened my mouth to speak, then I thought better of it. They'd have jumped down my throat if I'd told them about ghost girls popping out of the wallpaper. It would have sounded like a really crummy excuse.

"Well?" said Mrs. Sullivan.

"It *wasn't* us," said Mo. "Truly it wasn't!"

I don't think Mrs. Sullivan believed us.

She went off to bed muttering dark things about telling Mum and Dad, and letting them sort it out.

"Somebody'll have to pay for the damage!" was her parting shot.

"Well?" Mo said, when she'd gone.

"I didn't do it."

"And I didn't do it," said Mo.

"Mo," I said. "There's something I want to tell you. Will you sit still and believe me, because I'm telling the God's Honest Truth, though I didn't tell you before, because you'd only say I was making it up."

Then I told her.

All of it.

And I showed her the locket.

"You're kidding?" she asked.

"I'm not."

"Cross-your-heart-and-dare-to-die?"

"There," I said, doing it.

"Are you *sure*?"

"As sure as I'm sitting here."

"Och, Clare, come on!"

"It's true, honestly!"

"D'you expect me to tell *her* that?" asked Mo, nodding toward the door.

I shook my head.

"She wouldn't believe it for a minute," said Mo.

"It's not my fault," I said. "I didn't want any of this to happen."

"You're a great one for making things up, you know," said Mo. "But you've gone too far with this one. Nobody would believe this one!"

"I want *you* to," I said.

She didn't say anything for a long time.

"There's a ghost in this room? You're sticking to the story? You want me to believe *that*? You want me to tell Mrs. Sullivan and Mum and Dad that there's a ghost in our room?"

"I don't care who you tell, Mo. I just want *you* to believe it," I said.

I should never have told her. I knew it wouldn't work.

"Who else have you told?" she asked.

"The Canon."

"What did he say?"

"He said I had a vivid imagination. Something like that. That's what I think he meant, only he is too kind to say it that way. He went on about my age, and everything."

"Everything?"

"Because I was feeling a bit left out," I said. "Because you were off with your Mystery Man. He thought I was making a fuss because I had nothing better to do. He didn't say that, but that's what he meant."

"Well?" said Mo, not very kindly.

"I'm *not* making it up," I said.

Mo got into bed, but she didn't do her About-to-be-a-Sleeping-Beauty-Act.

"Well, now you've got attention, haven't you?" she said, sulkily. "Lots of it! They'll all be paying us attention. Mrs. Sullivan, and Mum and Dad. They'll all say we were carrying on together and bust the fireplace and we're supposed to say Oh-No-It-Wasn't-Us-It-Was-Clare's-Ghost."

"What else can we say?" I asked.

"You try it!" said Mo. "You go tomorrow after breakfast and explain to Mrs. Sullivan that there's a ghost in this house. You do it! I'm not! I don't want her to think I'm mad as well as bad."

There was a long silence.

"I will," I said. "It's the *truth*."

Mo lay down in bed.

"You DO believe it, don't you?" she said, in a worried voice.

70

"Yes," I said. "I do. I do because it is *true*."

"They'll all get thick at me for not staying round to play snotty games on the sand with you," she said bitterly. "You're *mean*. You don't want me to have any life of my own."

"I'm not interested in your life," I said.

"Oh, yes you are. You're *jealous*!" she said. "Just because I'm having a good time. Just because . . . well, just because."

She turned over with her back to me, and didn't say another word.

I didn't try speaking to her either.

12

"Do you know what I think?" Mo said, in the morning, after she'd made her bed. "I think you did it, and you're making up one of your stories to get out of it."

"Think what you like!" I said, because I had had enough of trying to persuade her. She didn't believe me, and that was all there was to it.

"I don't see why I should get into trouble with Mum and Dad and Mrs. Sullivan because of you!" Mo said, and she flounced off down the stairs.

That was a facer! I should have expected it, but for years and years Mo had been the person I talked to and the one I trailed after, I suppose. Now we were enemies with probably another confrontation to go through downstairs, when Mrs. Sullivan arrived with the breakfast.

"I'm moving you to separate rooms," was all she said, and she gave us a look.

"Good!" said Mo, when Mrs. Sullivan had gone out.

I didn't say anything. I concentrated on my cornflakes.

After breakfast, Mo cleared off, and I took the dishes down to the kitchen.

"Thank you," Mrs. Sullivan said, taking them from me.

"I'm sorry about last night, Mrs. Sullivan," I said.

She didn't say anything. She started doing the dishes, and I started drying, although she didn't ask me to.

"You look pale," she said, when we'd finished.

We went out to the back to get the washing in. We started unpegging the clothes from the line up by the barn. It was an awkward old line, high up, because otherwise the goats would have eaten everything. That's what Peter Archer told me, anyway.

"I'll be moving you into No. 7, now that Mr. Soraghan has left us," said Mrs. Sullivan. "Your sister can have the room at the back."

"There's no need," I said. I was afraid she would say she'd had to move us because we were causing trouble, and then she would ask Mum to pay for two singles, instead of a double, because we had two rooms.

She wouldn't do that, would she? She was supposed to be a friend of Mum's, and it was only an old fireplace. It wasn't as if we'd done any real damage.

"I think the room you're in is not the *right* room for you," she said.

The way she said it puzzled me. She didn't sound as if she was cross, or getting at me. What did she mean? What *could* she mean?

She was dropping the clothes pegs into a small dip scooped out in the stone at her feet, and I bent down to retrieve the pegs, with my mind going thirteen to the dozen. The clothes peg hole was an awkward shape, like a fish-hook, and one of the pegs caught in it. I jerked it free, and almost hit myself on the nose.

"Mind yourself!" she said.

I helped her carry the things back into the house, and stow them in the airing cupboard.

"Why do you want to move me out of that room, Mrs. Sullivan?" I asked.

I was taking the risk of getting a catalogue of my offences, or having my nose bitten off, but I felt safe enough. The *right* room . . .

She took a deep breath. Then she said, "I think you know."

Suddenly I got it. "*You* saw her too. You know she's . . . she's whatever she is."

"There's nothing to be frightened of," said Mrs. Sullivan, hurriedly. "She never *did* anything. I just *saw* her a few times, when I was about your age. I never told anybody. Daddy didn't like that sort of thing, d'you see? But I saw her. I know that."

"So did I," I said, and I've never felt so relieved in all my life. If somebody else had seen

74

the ghost girl, it meant I wasn't going straight round the bend!

"It's best to keep mum about a thing like that," said Mrs. Sullivan.

"I told the Canon," I said. "He doesn't believe me."

"You told the Canon? I never had the nerve to tell anybody. I was afraid of the fuss there'd be, and me carted off to hospital to have my head examined. There was nobody I could talk to, then. They'd have told me I was off my beano, if I'd let on."

"But you did *see* her, didn't you?" I said.

"I saw her."

"So did I."

We were repeating ourselves. The trouble was that she really didn't want to say anything, and I didn't know what to say. She seemed embarrassed about it, wanting away from the subject. In the end, she made an excuse and went out of the room. When she came back, she had a small silver chain with her, with a cross on it.

"You take that," she said. "You never know."

"I'm not afraid of her," I said. "I mean, thanks and everything but I don't really need this. I wouldn't know what to do with it."

"You'll come to no harm if you have that," said Mrs. Sullivan, firmly.

"And you'll let me stay in the room?"

"I will *not*!" said Mrs. Sullivan, and she wouldn't be talked out of it. All she'd say was: "Don't say a word to a living soul!"

I went back up to the room.

At least somebody believed me, even if the same somebody wouldn't own up that she did. The Canon couldn't argue with the broken fire-basket, and the hole in the back of the fireplace. I was looking forward to letting him explain that!

I looked at the fireplace.

The fire-basket must have been thrown hard to break in the back of the fireplace like that, I thought, and then I realised that it *couldn't* be . . . fire-baskets don't break through cement and plaster.

Maybe they *did*. I hadn't much experience of throwing fire-baskets at fireplaces.

Who threw it?

13

I spent most of the morning playing Krazy Golf
with Maxi. I was Jack Nicklaus and he was
Darth Vader, though I told him Darth Vader
didn't play golf. Darth Vader ended up as World
Champion of Bonecastle Krazy Golf and I had
to buy him a Star Wars ice cream.

If it had been ordinary putting I'd have
beaten him.

We went back to Garrison House for lunch,
and then the arrangement was that Mo would
take him after lunch.

"Marvellous!" she said, but she did it, and I
was free to go Canon-Hunting. I caught him on
the stairs, just when he was on his way to the
front door.

"Lucie Soraghan!" I said. "It's her. And
there's a bit of her hair!"

I showed him the compartment at the back of
the locket, the broken catch, the piece of hair and
the paper it was wrapped in.

"It means she was a *Soraghan*," I said. "Like
Mr. Soraghan. One of the Betrayer's family.
And that's her hair. Isn't it nice? It's all soft and
shiny, even though it's very old."

"Soraghan?" said the Canon.

"Like the Betrayer," I said.

"Lucie Soraghan, eh? Lucie Soraghan, who-are-you?" he asked.

"Lucie Soraghan," I said, impatiently. "Like it says on the bit of paper. The bit of paper was wrapped round the piece of hair, and they were hidden in the locket where nobody would find them. Only I did!"

He put the locket down on the hall-stand. "I'd need to talk to you about that," he said.

"Why?"

"That name and the picture don't fit each other," he said.

"It's Lucie Soraghan's hair, and that is Lucie Soraghan's picture," I said.

"I can't talk now," he said. "I'm called to the bungalow. I tell you what. I'm to be at the Parish House around three o'clock to sort a few books. Would you come there? There's something I can show you, that will explain what I'm trying to say better than anything else."

"All right," I said, not very enthusiastically.

As he went out the door, Peter Archer appeared up the path, coming in.

"Looking for me?" I said, and then I wished I hadn't because if he wasn't it would look as if I hoped he was.

"No," he said.

I felt a real fool, standing there on my famous feet as if I'd been waiting for Peter to come.

"You can give me a hand, if you like," he said, seeing my face.

"What doing?"

"I'm on fireplace fixing duty," he said, and then I noticed the bag of tools he had with him, and the drop of cement.

"What were you doing, busting up your fireplace?" he asked

"Oh, nothing," I said.

We went up to the room.

"Spread that paper for me," said Peter. "Then we'll have a look at it, will we?"

We spread some newspaper round the grate, and then Peter got down, and put his finger-tips inside the small hole in the back of the fireplace.

"I'd say one knock with a hammer should do that," he said, testing it. He closed his fist, and banged hard against the back of the fireplace with the side of his hand. There was a crack and a split ran right across the back of the fireplace. He took the hammer, and struck a light blow. The whole surface caved in.

It left a black hole there, about the size of a football.

Peter bent forward, and shoved his arm into it, up to the elbow. He felt about inside.

"It was only a light covering, a few bricks and mortar," he said. "Somebody threw it up in a hurry, I'd say."

He pulled his arm out.

"What's that?" I said.

In his hand there was a dusty bundle.

"It's mucky enough, whatever it is," he said.

I took it from him, and we dusted it off with the hearth brush. It was a small satchel, made of brown leather.

"Open it," he said.

The front was fastened with a brass lock. There was no sign of a key.

"I can't," I said.

"It doesn't look very strong," he said. "I'll tear it."

"No. Don't. It isn't ours, is it?"

"Who does it belong to?"

"Mrs. Sullivan, I suppose," I said. "It might be something to do with her family. Something *personal*, I mean."

In the back of my mind was the thought that if the girl I had seen wasn't a Soraghan – and the Canon seemed very definite about that – then she might be a Sullivan. I didn't want to go prying into somebody's family like that.

"We should give it to Mrs. Sullivan," I said.

Peter made a face. "I'll just give it a tug, that's all," he said, testing it with his fingers, "Look, it's rotten with age. It will pull apart."

"No," I said.

"All right," Peter said.

"I'm not being nasty," I said. "I mean, you found it. But it does belong to Mrs. Sullivan. We shouldn't interfere,"

We went downstairs. Mrs. Sullivan was out in the back, spraying the potatoes. She put down the watering can, and took the satchel.

"What's this?"

"It was tucked into the back of the fireplace, when I opened her up," said Peter. "There was a hidey hole in behind the bricks."

"What's in it?" asked Mrs. Sullivan.

"Clare said you had to look," said Peter, grinning at me.

"It is your property, isn't it?" I said. "I thought it might be something personal."

"Pull it open," said Mrs. Sullivan, when she had turned it over, and seen the lock.

Peter wrenched at the lock, which wouldn't give. Then we went back into the kitchen and he got some pliers and pulled at it, twisting the leather.

"Careful now, son," said Mrs. Sullivan. "Maybe it is money. You and me for the Bahamas! How's that?"

But it wasn't money.

"Papers!" said Mrs. Sullivan. "What's the use of that?"

"No use!" said Peter, sounding disappointed.

I took the papers from Mrs. Sullivan. Maybe there'd be a Treasure Map or instructions.

No such luck!

It was just lists.

They were clearly written out, in a dark ink on brittle paper. No doubt the heat of the fire had added to the brittleness over the years.

"It's in French," I said.

"Big deal," said Peter.

"It isn't all in French," I said. "There's a bit about Ballyshannon. And Single Street." I turned over a page. "Donegal Town too . . . look there, at the side. It's some kind of inventory, divided up under place names."

"There's letters as well," said Mrs. Sullivan, who'd been thumbing through the sheaf in my hand. "Look at that! Did you ever?"

"It's a cipher!" I said, with visions of my treasure bit.

I read the top line. My French isn't up to much, but even I could manage that:

RECIT DES AFFAIRES MILITAIRES DU NORD OUEST DE L'IRLANDE APRES JUILLET DIX SEPT CENT QUARANTE QUATRE.

"Military Affairs in North West Ireland," I said. "1744."

"It'll not be red hot news then, whatever it is!" Peter said.

"It's an odd thing to find up your chimney," said Mrs. Sullivan.

"This was a military place, wasn't it?" I said. "This house, I mean. That is why it is called Garrison House. Captain Murray, the one who hanged Father Maury, used this house as his headquarters. Isn't that right? These would be lists of his, maybe."

"I suppose so," said Peter.

"We could find out, if we get someone to look at them," I said. "I can't make much sense of it."

"This was Murray's place," said Peter. "But he took his orders from Donegal town."

I was fed up. After all that had happened, I'd been expecting something BIG to turn up, not a few crummy old lists of military things.

"Take them to the Canon," said Mrs. Sullivan. "He will tell you all about them."

"I'll do that," I said.

"Walk up to the Parish House and you'll just about catch him," said Mrs. Sullivan.

"I'd better finish off upstairs," said Peter.

"Keep young Clare company, Peter," she said.

I went red!

"All square for the double dating, eh?" said Mrs. Sullivan.

"What did she mean, the double dating?" I said, as we walked up Murray's Hill.

"Your Maureen and Henry," he said.

Henry Archer! So Peter's big brother was the Mystery Man.

"But we're not dating," I said.

"It would be kind of handy, wouldn't it?" he said.

"I don't do dating," I said.

"Why not?"

"*Just*," I said.

Neither of us said anything for a long time.

"When I was a kid," I said. "I thought this was *Maury's* Hill, after the Hanged Priest. I thought they'd hanged him at the bawn, because the soldiers were there, and called the hill after him."

"Why don't you do dating?" Peter said.

"Nobody's asked me," I said.

I knew I was going all red again. I wish I didn't go red. Other people don't go red. I must be the reddest-going person in the whole world.

"Supposing somebody did," he said.

"I'll *suppose* about it when it happens," I said.

We went past the Church of Ireland, set square and rather grand in its graveyard. I felt a bit odd, going past our own church like that, on my way to see a Catholic Priest. I could have gone in to see Mr. Claremorris, if he hadn't been such a drip.

"Why would it be *French*?" I asked.

"What?"

"The lists. Why would they be in French? It was an *English* garrison, after all. Why should the lists be in *French*?"

"I don't know," Peter said.

I was half fed up with him, and half not, although the half-not half was the bigger half any day! Just the same, if he wanted to ask something he should ask it, and if he didn't want to ask something he shouldn't have started asking it in the first place. Anyway, I leave that sort of thing to people who think they are gorgeous, like our Mo.

"I'm going into the Canon's now," I said, stopping at the gate. "Are you coming?"

"I'd better get back," he said.

"The Canon won't bite your nose off," I said.

"I have the fireplace to fix," he said.

"See you then."

"Right," he said.

He didn't go.

He just stood there, looking sheepish.

"Are you going?" I asked.

"I'd better go."

I smiled at him. I mean, I liked him. He's not bad. Only I couldn't stand out in the middle of the road smiling at him all day, could I? If he wanted to ask something he should ask it.

"If you wanted to . . ." I started, and then I stopped.

"If I wanted to what?" he said.

"I don't know. Whatever you wanted to do," I said.

Long silence!

"I'd better go back then," he said.

Off he went.

I bet old Mo never had to put up with a performance like that. I wish I was as nice looking as Mo, with hair and everything.

Maybe my big feet put him off.

I went off to my real boyfriend, the Canon, wishing I *was* Mo . . . though mind you, if I'd been Mo, I'd have been nicer to me.

14

I tried the bell, but it wasn't working. Maybe they had disconnected the electricity. I pushed the door, and it opened.

"Canon?" I called. "Canon?"

There was no response.

I wasn't going to stand around on my famous feet looking like a prune, so I went in.

The house was weird, with no furniture in it. There was just a straw mat in the hall, and white patches on the walls where the pictures had been.

"Canon?" I went into his study.

No desk. No bookcases. No clock. No mirror. His books were in orderly piles by the window, along with his papers in their neat green folders.

The room was still alive, but only just. It was as if the rest of the house had withered away, concentrating all the life that was still in it in the one spot. I suppose it might be like that to die, feeling life ebb away, until there is just the one little room left.

I found what I was looking for – Father Maury's Journals. Strictly speaking I shouldn't have been poking around in the Canon's things without his permission, but I didn't have to poke, because they were right on top of one of the piles.

The writing wasn't like the *'Recit des Affaires Militaires'*, which was a bit of a blow. I'd been doing detective work in my mind and come up with the idea that it would be the same handwriting, and that I'd be able to prove Father Maury was a spy for the French and show the Canon that Captain Murray was quite right to have him hanged. If you believe in hanging people at all, that is. I wouldn't like to be hanged, personally.

"You let yourself in," the Canon said.

I nearly jumped out of my skin. He had come in very quietly, though there wasn't much of him to make a noise at the best of times.

"You're reading Father Maury?" he said.

"I was just wondering," I said. "Father Maury would have been a fugitive to begin with, wouldn't he? A Catholic Priest in those days might have been a prisoner in Garrison House sometime, mightn't he?"

My idea was that Father Maury had hidden the papers behind the fireplace, but the big difficulty was what he'd be doing there in the first place. Perhaps he hadn't been taken straight off to be hanged. Maybe he'd been brought to Garrison House and hidden the stuff while he was there. It didn't seem very likely.

"No, you're wrong there," the Canon said. "Captain Murray at Garrison House was a decent man by all accounts. They say it was live and let live with him and Father Maury, not like some of the military. That is why he had to act so quickly when he found out about Maury. It must have gone hard to have Donegal town getting on to him with the news that they'd taken a Jacobite messenger, and the message was for Maury. It put the Captain in a dangerous position, and he had a wife and daughter to consider."

"I thought Eoin Soraghan betrayed Father Maury," I said. "Isn't that why he is called The Betrayer?"

"Soraghan was a sneak thief," said Canon Roche, twisting his mouth. "A man who would skulk around and steal from a Priest, and a Priest about to die on his enemy's scaffold at that! Soraghan waited until the soldiers dragged Father Maury away, and then he slithered in like a slug to see what he could feed on! The sorrow is that he got the crucifix, a thing Father Maury had brought with him from France."

"*France?*" I said, brightening up. The stuff behind the chimney was all in French! Maybe I was on to something after all.

"Maury had been in France, like a good many other Catholics at that time," said the Canon. "He came back here to do what he could for men like Soraghan, and Soraghan was a man who betrayed his Faith, and his own people, for the sake of a golden cross!"

You could have set it to violin music, almost! He saw me grinning and he caught himself.

"But he was killed, wasn't he?" I said. "The soldiers caught Soraghan and killed him, so his stealing didn't do him much good."

"They took him to Ballyshannon, but by that time he'd managed to get rid of the crucifix, and no doubt he'd had his day on the proceeds. He must have had a brass neck. They say he refused to open his mouth about Priest or cross, for all they did to him, before he died!"

"Why?" I asked.

"*Why?*"

"Why should he? I mean, I can understand why Father Maury wouldn't give away the names of his fellow conspirators, but why would Eoin Soraghan not say where the crucifix was?"

"Pig headed, I suppose," said the Canon. "He was an island man, you know. But then again, maybe not. I don't profess to know the answer to that one. Why do you think?"

"I don't know. I'm asking you."

"Would it be giving him too much grace to say that the man had the decency to go to his death without taking anyone with him, I wonder?" said the Canon. "An accomplice, perhaps, who had the crucifix? That would likely be it. It may be that he had some shred of good feeling left in him, despite the black name. He was a big man on the island, one time, a man they would have looked up to. A man who would once have had pride in himself. It may be that that came to his aid in the end."

"Perhaps the cross was very valuable, and he'd sold it for a lot of money to help his starving family," I said, thinking of the little houses on Tomas Mor.

"It would take a lot more than 'valuable' to keep a man's mouth shut when the soldiers had him! They say the messenger they caught that gave Maury's name was half dead when he cried it and I don't doubt that the treatment meted out to Eoin Soraghan was the same. Captain Murray was in a delicate position. He'd already been in trouble for not fully enforcing the laws against the Catholic Church, and the arrest of Father Maury must have been a bad blow. He needed all the information he could get, quickly, and I don't doubt that it was extracted, in the manner of the times. I suppose Soraghan might have kept his mouth shut to protect the rest of his family, if some of them were involved, but if it was only a question of the money, he'd have told."

"I suppose so," I said.

"It was your so-called Lucie Soraghan we were to sort out, wasn't it?" he said, leaning against the window frame. It was all there was to lean against.

"That's right," I said. "But there's something else!" And I showed him the papers from the satchel. "Mrs. Sullivan said I was to let you take a look at them," I said.

The Canon became very excited. "You have a real find there!" he said, thumbing through them. "That's great stuff. You may leave them with me, child, till I see what I make of them."

"It says about 1744 on one of them," I said. "So they must be just before the '45 rebellion, mustn't they?"

"Isn't that *fan-tab-ul-ous*!" he muttered, as if I wasn't there.

I was very polite and well behaved and everything. I didn't interrupt him.

"Did I forget you?" he said. "It is Lucie you want to know about, isn't it? Your ghost! Hold on now."

He got up from the window, and went down on the floor, where he worked his way through his folders. "I have the local records, or rather I had them photocopied for me."

He pulled out a photocopied sheet, and handed it to me.

"What's this?" I asked, blankly.

"Eoin Soraghan, that you're so keen on. He was a young man, not married, but he came from a strong family on the island. He was a leader, before his downfall. This is a copy of a petition about landing rights at the Milk Harbour. It is directed to the authorities in Dublin, no less. I've no doubt Father Maury had a hand in dreaming up that idea! But the thing I want to show you is *that*!"

He prodded his finger at the bottom of the photocopy.

$\int$

EOIN SORAGHAN   His mark

"They were all illiterate, on the island," Canon Roche said. "I don't think that there would have been one of them who could put pen to paper. They'd be rough souls, d'you see, and fine cannon fodder for an uprising, if you could get them involved. Which wouldn't be easy, because they had a world of their own, out there! The Tomas Beg men are the same to this day, though they can read and write and they have electricity and what not. The island and its affairs come first."

"If they were illiterate, who wrote this?" I said.

"*Somebody*, but not Eoin Soraghan," said the Canon. "And not your Lucie Soraghan either, if there was one. You can bet your boots on that."

"Why?"

"The locket picture. She's a pretty flower, that one, with a low cut dress and high hair and rosy cheeks. Can you see that article living in a stone cottage on Tomas Mor? Evening dress and all? No. Whoever she was, she was no Soraghan. And if she had been a Soraghan, she wouldn't have been able to read and write. If Eoin couldn't, and he was the top man around, then nobody else could either."

"I see," I said.

"The bit of hair doesn't belong to the picture," said the Canon. "Two separate things. Now if the bit of hair does *not* belong to the picture, and dates from later than 1744 you are into National Schooling and so on. You'd find plenty of Lucie Soraghans who could write then. Why one of them should hide her hair in a twist of paper with her name on it, and put it in the back of an old locket I don't know, but still. You can forget about a Jacobite Lucie Soraghan horsing around the islands. Lucie here is nothing to do with Eoin and his misdeeds, nothing at all."

"Unless she *could* write," I said, not to be put off as easily as that. "She might . . . she might have been some soldier's mistress or something, and picked it up."

"Most of the soldiers couldn't write either," said the Canon, patiently.

"They could probably sign their names, though," I said. "Somebody could have taught

Lucie to write her name. Maybe Father Maury did! Maybe he *visited* the island and taught her?"

"That girl in your picture is a bold biddy!" said the Canon. "You've only to look at her to know she was never brought up in a shack on Tomas Mor!"

15

It was very cold. Not I'm-about-to-see-a-ghost-cold, the other sort.

Like an idiot I'd taken Maxie down to the beach, after tea. He'd gone rock climbing, but I didn't fancy it, and anyway I wanted to keep an eye out in case Peter was out for a walk, or something.

I went down by the lip of the tide, with the town far behind me, and looked out at Eoin Soraghan's island, Tomas Mor, Big Tom, the Isle of the Betrayer. Actually, I wasn't sure I was looking at Big Tom. It could have been Tomas Beg, but I was in a romantic mood, so I decided I would stand there and think it was Tomas Mor, and then it would be.

The Canon was right. Of course the Canon was right. No Soraghan would have been running about the island dressed in low cut evening dresses, with piled up hair.

"Maxie? Maxie? Time we were getting home, Maxie!"

He came slithering down the rocks, on the wet side. That would do good work on his trousers.

"Look at you, Maxie!" I said, in disgust.

We went up on to the promenade, and along past the Hanged Priest. It isn't a statue. It's a big lump of rock with his name on it, and a cross. It had a few other bits as well, added in more recent times in white paint.

BRITS OUT I.R.A. PROVO RULE

Things hadn't changed much.

Father Maury and Soraghan and Captain Henry Murray and the Canon and Mrs. Sullivan, we were all part of it, the same old thing. On the side of the bridge someone had painted an Irish tricolour, green and white and orange. The idea was to symbolise the green and orange coming together.

Somebody had splashed up

DEATH TO ALL INFORMERS

in big white letters alongside it.

We live in the North, so I suppose that makes *me* a Brit. Dad has a British passport, but he could have an Irish one. He says I must choose for myself, when I grow up. I'm Irish, *and* a Brit, and I bet I am a better Irish person than the one who wrote 'Brits Out' on Father Maury's stone, and a better Brit than some of the Protestants in Belfast, attacking Catholics.

"Come on, Maxie," I said.

We went on up Murray's Hill.

"When I grow up, I'm going to leave Ireland," I told the Canon, when we got in the house.

"Oh no," he said. "You stay."

"Why should I?" I asked.

"Because somebody's got to see both sides," he said.

"I'm going to America," said Maxie. "I'm going to be an astronaut."

"When he goes buzzing over the top of us, he'll see the same old fight going on!" Mo said, looking up from her book.

"Will you stay, Mo?" I asked her.

"No," she said. "I'm sick of people killing people."

I don't know if she meant it. I don't know if I mean it. Maybe I'll go, and maybe I won't.

There's a fierce bit of me that doesn't want to go, because it is my land. I've as much right to it as all the people in the secret armies, with all their fancy initials, going around scrawling their names on graves.

I took Maxie up to bed, read him a story, and left him.

I didn't go downstairs again, and I didn't go to my new room. I went down the corridor and slipped into the other room.

I sat down in the big chair and *waited*, with the light off and the curtains back, looking out through the window at the sea, toward the islands.

Nothing happened!

I knew why.

My own mind was getting in the way. I was full of my stories, filled up to the brim.

No Ghost Girl.

No Eoin Soraghan.

No time-slip, where I looked out of the window and saw the soldiers leading Father Maury away and tried to rescue him. It would all have been like that, and a great adventure, if I'd been in a TV serial, and much, much simpler than it was in real life.

In real life Father Maury was a Provo, and Eoin was an Informer, and Captain Murray was a Brit and the Ghost Girl, Lucie, if she *was* Lucie . . . what was she?

Maybe she was just like me, caught in the middle.

They were all dead, and it hadn't made any difference.

I should have been away out of the room, with somebody alive, like Peter. Maybe Peter, but he'd never asked me.

In the end I took my big feet off to bed, in my own room, away from all the trouble.

16

All of a sudden, it seemed to be over. No Ghost Girl, no secret hiding places, no being-a-detective.

The world had gone flat.

I settled down to Maxie-minding and fighting with Mo and helping Mrs. Sullivan with the dishes and I felt absolutely cheated.

I didn't try sitting in the room again, but I got out a library book on one of the Canon's tickets. It was all about 18th Century Ireland, and I got bored with it. Then I had another go at Mrs. Sullivan, but she was very stilted and uptight on the subject of spectres she'd seen in the long, long ago when she was my age, and absolutely determined to forget all about broken fireplaces.

It was a total wash-out!

I had to do something, so I thought I'd take Maxie and Michael for a picnic.

"Will you?" Mrs. Sullivan said, when I asked her about sandwiches, and she gave me a knowing look.

I thought it was a good idea, but the Archers had all gone to Ballyshannon.

"Picnic?" said Mo.

"Up on the hill behind the Church of Ireland, there's a great view."

"Big deal!" Mo said.

I asked the Canon if he would like to come, but he was too busy doing Parish things with the new man from the bungalow.

"We'll go on our own, Maxie," I said, and off we went.

"You be Alan Breck Stewart and I'll be wicked Campbells and you can ambush me," I told him.

"*Who?*" said Maxie.

"Never mind," I said, because I wasn't going to recite the whole of *Kidnapped* for him. "You be Hans Solo and I'll be Darth Vader and you can ambush me."

"I'd rather be Darth Vader," he said.

We Darth Vadered it right up the hill, through the Church of Ireland graveyard and over the wall on to the hillside.

It was nice.

The sun was out and we were having fun. Maxie was having one of his good days. He fell and cut his leg and he didn't even yell, once he found out that I wasn't going to tell him off for mucking up his trousers.

"I'll clean them up before Mum comes," I told him.

That cheered him up.

I think he was missing Mum quite a bit,

although he had been very good about it. I was missing her and Dad.

"You be . . . you be the Daleks, and I'll be Doctor Who and you can ambush me!" I said, with the idea that I'd be Doctor Who sitting down and he could creep around the boulders exterminating.

"I don't want to," he said.

That was a relief.

"What do you want to do?" I asked.

"Eat!" he said.

Lettuce and tomato inside buttered baps, with an orange each to wash it down, and chocolate biscuits. Mrs. Sullivan had done her bit. When we'd finished eating I gave Maxie a piggy-back up to the top of the slope, and we looked out over the sweep of the land. It was mostly rocky outcrops, but the bungalows spoiled it.

"Now what?" said Maxie.

"Now I'm sitting down," I said. "You do what you like, but don't get killed in the process, okay?"

Maxie wandered off, looking a bit lost. He'd have had a better time if Michael Archer had come with us, and perhaps Peter would have come as well. I'm not saying that that was the idea that I'd started off with, but I'm not saying that it wasn't!

I lay down flat on a big grey rock and closed my eyes.

Maury, not Murray . . . the name of the hill. What had brought that into my mind? Supposing the Priest who was hanged was really Captain Murray's *brother*, only using a French version of the name? Supposing . . .?

I didn't want to *suppose*. I wanted to lie there in the sun enjoying myself.

An S like a fish hook. *Eoin Soraghan, his mark.*

There was something at the edge of my mind, something that wouldn't quite come to the centre.

Eoin. Eoin.

The name started to repeat in my head.

I opened my eyes, to break the spell. What was I doing getting all worked up about Eoin Soraghan, all of a sudden?

Eoin. Eoin.

I could *hear* his name in my head, but it wasn't my voice I could hear saying it.

Eoin. Eoin.

"Stop it!" I said.

It stopped, but the moment I settled back on the rock, it started again.

Eoin. Eoin.

I got up. Obviously I was having a nervous breakdown through too much Maxie-minding and ghost talk. I didn't want to have my life interfered with by something that had happened hundreds of years ago.

Eoin. Eoin.

It was the weirdest thing. I could actually *hear* the voice, although it wasn't really there at all.

I didn't like it.

"Maxie!" I shouted. "Maxie. Time to go!"

Maxie came down over the rocks, and on past me.

Eoin. Eoin.

I was all fuzzed up.

"Hold on, Maxie!" I shouted, but he was already over the back wall of the church, and skidding away between the graves waving a stick he'd picked up somewhere.

"Maxie!"

He'd be out on the road, and get himself killed. Actually he wouldn't, Maxie is good with roads, for his age, but I didn't want to get too far behind him.

Eoin. Eoin. Eoin. Eoin.

It was a kind of whispering, in my head.

I started to run, but it was a mistake, because I was going downhill, and it was difficult to keep my balance, especially with my head all fuzzy.

Eoin. Eoin. Eoin. Eoin. Eoin.

"Maxie!" I shouted. "MAXIE!"

Eoin. Eoin.

"Maxie! Maxie!"

Eoin and *Maxie* were tumbled together as words in my brain, but I was the one shouting Maxie and the Eoin was coming from someone else, although the someone else was *inside* me.

I came over the graveyard wall, stumbled, got to my feet, and shouted "MAXIE!"

Maxie didn't come.

The girl came gliding towards me, over the thick grass. She was all mixed up in the bright, blinding light of the sun.

The same grey dress, the lace cuffs, the cold, drawn waxwork face.

Eoin. Eoin. Eoin. Eoin. Eoin. Eoin.

"Eoin!" Now I was saying it, as well.

She stopped, and the sunlight seemed to shimmer round the edges of her body.

'*So she's solid,*' I thought. '*They aren't supposed to be.*'

Eoin. Eoin. Eoin.

I could hardly breathe. I was frightened for me and frightened for Maxie, in case he would suddenly see her.

Eoin. Eoin. Eoin.

The light got brighter and brighter and brighter, burning into me, and I had to close my eyes. When I opened them, it was over, and there was wee Maxie, looking down at me.

"Did you fall over?" he asked.

"I . . . I . . ."

"Did you hurt yourself, Clare?" he asked, anxiously.

"I'm all right, Maxie," I said.

I got to my feet.

I had a terrible, splitting headache, the worst

in the world, as if my head was about to divide up in two parts.

"Are you *sick*, Clare?" Maxie asked.

"No, Maxie, I'm fine," I said. "Just give me a minute to get steady."

I went forward a few steps, and knelt down. There were weeds and long grasses all over the flat stone, but I cleared them back.

> Here Lies in her Resting Place
> Lucie Murray,
> My Dear Child,
> Taken in her XVII year by God's Will.
> This stone laid by
> Henry Murray. A.D. 1746.
> Also Captain Henry Murray,
> departed this life A.D. 1752.

"Are we going home now, Clare?" asked Maxie. I took him by the hand.

Lucie *Murray*.

She was seventeen, and she died, and she loved Eoin.

Lucie Murray loved Eoin Soraghan.

I knew because, just for those few moments, Lucie Murray had been *in* my mind, calling his name.

Eoin. Eoin. Eoin.

Like that.

Her voice, still calling him, after all those years.

17

Canon Roche sat back on his chair, and frowned at me. I'd collared him after tea in Garrison House.

"It is a grand story," he said. "Let me summarise now, just to see that I have it right. Your imagination is too much for an old fellow to keep up with."

"It's not imagination!" I said, impatiently. "I've thought a lot about it, and this time I have put the pieces together, and they make sense. I *know* I have."

"Well, what you *know* and what I know might not be exactly the same thing."

I could have wrung his neck! Not *really*, but it was awfully irritating. I was certain because, in that moment, coming over the graveyard wall, calling for Eoin, I had *been* her. I'd felt what she felt, and it wasn't what I'd expected at all.

"To begin again," the Canon said. "Your Lucie Soraghan wasn't Lucie Soraghan at all. She was Lucie Murray . . ."

"She *might* have been Lucie Soraghan," I butted in. "They might have been secretly married."

"Ah!" he said. "Another bit to the story? Gretna Green, is it?":

"I don't know about that," I said, quickly. "We can leave out the secret marriage bit. It doesn't matter. She just *called* herself that, to please Eoin when she gave him the locket. I mean, they *could* have been secretly married, I suppose. Father Maury could have done it, but they didn't have to be. She only had to be in love with him."

"It is a big only," Canon Roche said, wearily.

I'd *been* her, so I knew what she felt, but there was no use trying to convince him of that.

"I don't see *why* it is a big only," I said.

"She was sixteen," he said. "Seventeen when she died in '46. That makes her sixteen, no, fifteen, in '44."

"People of fifteen can be in love," I said. "Juliet was fourteen, wasn't she? And she's in the most famous love story in the world."

"Give or take Adam and Eve," said Canon Roche. "Still, forgetting about the secret marriage, if there was one, I'd prefer to forget it, forgetting that, and forgetting she was only fifteen, and forgetting that she was the Garrison Captain's daughter, and forgetting that Eoin was a bit of a peasant . . ."

"You said he was a leader on the island," I said.

"The island was a hard place. It still is. I told

you young ladies in evening dresses wouldn't be having soirées there."

"Why did she give him the locket, then?" I said. "If she didn't love him, why did she give him the locket with her hair in it?"

"*Did* she give him the locket?" asked the Canon.

I was up against a brick wall. He didn't believe me.

"Maury and Murray sound the same," I said, ploughing on. "I know, because I used to think it was Maury's Hill, not Murray's. That alters a lot, doesn't it?"

"*What* does it alter?" he asked.

"*Everything!*" I said.

The Canon gave a sigh. I think he was regretting getting into the conversation. He looked tired out, and even older than usual. I should have shut up, I suppose, but it didn't seem fair. I wanted to explain it all.

"Look," he said. "You're trying to persuade me that Lucie Murray was a Jacobite agent."

"Not Lucie," I said. "Eoin. Eoin Soraghan! Her lover."

"What was Lucie, then?" he said.

"Lucie was like me," I said. "Caught in the middle. She just wanted to be in love with him, but he was mixed up in the rising, and plotting against her father, with the French."

"Oh yes," said the Canon. "Eoin would be a

dab hand at letter writing, particularly in French!"

"He wouldn't," I said. "But *she* would. She was educated. Her father had been all over the place. Lucie wrote it out for Eoin and perhaps she gave him information as well, I don't know. They were in love, that is the important thing. And then when the messenger was caught and being tortured he shrieked out 'Murray' before they killed him and they thought: 'That's it, Maury! He's the Priest up there. It must be Maury.' And then they sent off from Donegal town for his head. Captain Murray got the word, but his daughter managed to warn Eoin, and Eoin went to Father Maury to warn him, but Eoin was too late. Father Maury didn't say anything, because if he said what he knew it would have come out about Lucie, and she would have been hanged instead of him."

"By her father," said Canon Roche.

"Yes, I expect so. By her father."

"Do you know, to hear you tell it, I could almost believe it myself!" he said.

"But you don't!" I said.

"I don't," he agreed.

"She was in love. She was caught in the middle, between Eoin and her father," I said. "That's why it was so awful for her."

"That's the way it is in your head, child," he said. "You have a high octane imagination.

Listen to me, now, Clare Campbell. Leaving aside all your ghostie stories . . ."

"Why?" I said. We couldn't leave them aside. They were *it*. It was because of seeing her, and then *being* her for just that moment, that I knew.

"Because they are just ghostie stories," he said. "That's why! Leaving aside your ghostie stories, what have we? A few papers in the back of a bricked up fireplace."

"In *French*. In *her* room. In the Captain's own house!" I broke in. "You're not saying the Captain was the spy, are you?"

"You can't prove it was her room," he said. "You can't prove Lucie Murray was ever *in* the room."

"It was her house. She lived here with her father," I said.

"Even allowing that the papers are what you think, you can't prove Lucie met Soraghan, let alone loved him."

"She gave him the locket, with her hair, and she used his name, Lucie *Soraghan*. That means she must have loved him, mustn't she?"

"Ah!" he said. "These mixed marriages!" It was meant as a joke. The Canon isn't like that, but I *hated* it just the same.

"They loved each other," I said. "What religion they were didn't make any difference."

"It makes a whale of difference round these parts," said the Canon.

111

"It's all any of you care about!" I said.

"You know that's not true," he said.

"I sometimes wonder!" I said.

There was a long silence. He stirred himself. I think if he hadn't put a foot wrong about the mixed marriage he might have gone off and called it a day. My Mum and Dad are *mixed*, but then my Mum was a Scottish Catholic and that doesn't count. The only real Catholics are Irish ones, though they'll allow the Pope in, so long as he's old-fashioned. No wonder I get in a muddle about what side I'm supposed to be on. We're all Church of Ireland now, because my Grannie Campbell made a fuss.

"You say that Lucie Murray, the Captain's daughter, conspired *against* her father. Ireland's answer to Mati Hari. As far as I'm concerned, if that picture is Lucie Murray, she's no more than a bold looking piece of furniture, in a gown that shows too much of her upstairs."

"That's just a picture," I said. "She was all dressed up for that, to please her father. She wasn't like that at all. She was sad, and muddled up between the two of them, Eoin and her father. Eoin was killed and I think she pined away and died of a broken heart."

"Great stuff!" he said, getting to his feet. "I'm tired. I'm for my bed. You'll have to excuse me, child."

"I'm not finished yet!" I said.

112

He looked as if he was going to get mad.

"It *matters* to me," I said. "You said I could talk to you . . . now I'm doing it."

He sat down again.

"Talk," he said.

"Well, I've told you it, haven't I?" I said.

"You got hold of the picture in the locket," he said. "Then you worked back until you'd persuaded yourself that she looked like someone you'd imagined. You described the girl you'd seen to me, before you got the locket, and she was nothing like the locket picture, was she? That knocks the bottom out of that!"

"Eoin had been killed," I said. "I'm not surprised she looked a bit off colour. She loved him, can't you understand that? Lucie Murray loved Eoin Soraghan, no matter if he was the wrong religion and couldn't write his name and was against her father."

"Real life isn't like that," the Canon said.

"Real life is just like that!" I said. "People do fall in love, and they do incredible things, because they are in love."

"Incredible is about it," he agreed. "Calm down now. You're getting over-excited. I should never have passed remarks about mixed marriages and so on. I didn't mean anything by it, you understand?"

"It isn't Mum and Dad I'm annoyed about," I

said. "I'm annoyed because you won't believe me."

"We'll go over it again," said the Canon. A little spot of red had appeared on his cheek, just where the creases were. "*Now*. You described someone to me who looked quite different from the girl in the locket, didn't you? Can we start with that?"

"I've explained that!" I almost shouted it.

"Have you?" he asked.

"Mrs. Sullivan saw her too," I said. "Mrs. Sullivan saw her when Mrs. Sullivan was my age. Only she just *saw* Lucie, nothing else happened."

"If she did, you're the only one she's told it to," he said.

"She didn't tell anyone, because she thought no one would believe her!" I said. "She tries to pass it off as a joke now."

"She has a Guest House to keep," said the Canon.

"Ghosts are good for Guest Houses," I said. "She could make a fortune if it got into the papers."

"I doubt if that is the sort of fortune Mrs. Sullivan wants to make," said the Canon. "Whatever you say about that she won't back up your story. So you are on your own, girl."

"Oh, yes," I said. "And when I grow up everybody will believe everything. I'm just at a difficult stage, that's what everyone says. But this is not . . . Oh, what's the use?"

"Don't get angry," said the Canon. "Listen to me. If you had one single bit of concrete evidence, one bit of evidence that would back up your story . . . but it is all just imaginings, isn't it?"

I didn't say a word.

"Go and tell the boyfriend, young Peter," he said, in what was meant to be a kindly voice.

"It is none of Peter's business, and he's not my boyfriend, for your information!" I said.

"Find me one shred of evidence that will connect Eoin Soraghan with this place and with the Captain's daughter . . . that's all I'm asking you. You won't do it! He was an islander, he was maybe a rebel, he was a man who betrayed his own kind, a man who stole from a Priest on the scaffold. He took the crucifix, and he hid it, and he got caught. That's all there is to Eoin's story. No love interest. No sign that she ever knew him, let alone helped him."

"I suppose there isn't," I said.

"It's a nice story," he said. "But that is all it is."

He went off upstairs.

I sat downstairs, watching the bust TV set for a late newsflash from 1744, giving all the latest developments from Bonecastle.

Needless to say it didn't come on.

Lucie had got *into* me. I'm not on about being possessed, or anything like that. She wasn't going to get me to take a big knife and cut up my friends and relations like people in the horror films.

It wasn't like that at all.

It wasn't a good feeling, either.

She was all sadness and confusion, and there was no way in which I could work it out for her.

I didn't want to be her Thought Police, but somehow I'd been elected!

18

"Your boyfriend is out the back!" Mo said. "He's pretending to play games with Maxie, but *we* know who he's waiting for."

"Shut up, Mo!" I said, putting down my toast.

"Oh la-la!" she said, and she minced out of the room, doing her wiggle.

"You're the one for boyfriends!" I shouted after her. "What about big brother Henry?"

"I never fancied Henry Archer," she said. "Henry's a creep."

"He wasn't a creep a few days ago," I said. "He was the stars in your eyes!"

"That's all you know," she said, sounding humpy.

Henry Archer had given her the push! Serve her right.

I gave her a hundred to get out of the way, and then I went out to the back, where Peter and Maxie were carrying on up at the bawn.

"Hi," I said.

"Hullo," Peter said. "I'm playing with Maxie."

"That's nice for you," I said.

I went over the garden wall and up to the

bawn, and sat down by the washing line. I'd
come out, hadn't I? If that was what he wanted
he could do something about it!

Michael Archer came over the fence. He
didn't climb over it, Peter lifted him.

"You play with Maxie, Michael," Peter said,
and he walked up the back towards me.

"How was Ballyshannon?" I said.

"Same as ever," he said. "How did you know
we were there?"

"A little bird told me," I said. I didn't want
him thinking I was checking up every time he
moved, but I'd let myself in for it.

"We were fetching the Canon's clock from Mr.
Bannon," he said.

"Bannon?" I said. "Bannon from Ballyshannon? The dealer from the Auction?"

"It's the old clock from the Parish House,"
Peter said, sitting down beside me — not *too* close!
"Mr. Bannon had her down to Symns in Dublin
to get her going again. Cormac Crilly and the
Legion of Mary are presenting it to the Canon,
so that he'll have something to remember us by
in Mayo."

"And I never even got a bid in!" I said. "Fool
I would have been, wouldn't I? Bidding against
the town."

"What?"

"Oh, never mind," I said.

"We got the clock," he said.

Long silence.

My big feet were right out in front of me. I moved, and tucked them in, and then . . .

z . . . o . . . n . . . k! BINGO!

I crouched down over it, my fingers working at the edges. It was the clothes peg stone, the stone with the fish hook design cut in it.

$$\int$$

S . . . Eoin's sign!

Eoin Soraghan, his mark.

"Are you all right?" Peter asked. "What's the matter?"

"Fetch a trowel or a crowbar or something, quick!" I said. "I can't raise this thing on my own."

"Raise it?" he said. "What for?"

"Will you just do it?" I said, exasperated. I'd snagged my fingernail, trying to hook it down the side.

"You're bleeding," he said.

"Never mind the bleeding. Get some old thing that will help me raise this stone!" I said.

Peter shrugged and made a face, and then he ambled over to the fence and straddled it.

"Get a move on," I said.

"Keep your hair on!" He didn't look too pleased.

"Can we dig too?" said Maxie.

"I'm not digging," I said. "Just scraping!"

"You're daft," said Maxie.

"Give us the trowel thing!" I said, as Peter came back over the fence with Mo's Henry. Peter gave it to me, and they stood over me as I went at the stone.

"Let me do that," Henry said, in an I'm-taking-charge voice.

"I will not," I said.

It took a crowbar in the end, with Henry and Peter both levering on it and me working with the trowel.

We eased the stone up.

"What's all the fuss about?" said Henry.

"It's an old bag," said Peter.

I paid no heed.

I was working at the draw thong, with the point of the trowel, because I was too impatient to wait for a knife. It was rotten, and when I tugged, it snapped and the bag fell open.

There was an oblong box inside, with the initials L.M. engraved on it in spidery writing.

Lucie! Lucie Murray! L.M!

I opened the lid. The catch was rusty, but no old catch was going to stop me when I'd got that far.

The crucifix gleamed in the sunlight. I touched it, and lifted it from the velvet cloth that had held it for two hundred years.

For a minute, I didn't feel a thing. I was quite

empty, exhausted, as if something had gone out of me. Then I saw the slim green journal, with '1744' on the cover.

"What is it?" Peter asked.

"These are Father Maury's," I said. "Eoin and Lucie hid them here, where the soldiers would never look for them."

"Who hid them?"

"Peter," I said. "Peter, will you run and get the Canon for me! No hold on a minute. I'll get him myself, if I have to turf him out of bed to do it. I want to see his face."

I ran off down the slope toward Garrison House, with the box in my hands and a big glow inside me.

One shred of evidence . . . I'd got him his evidence. Now he would listen to me, now he'd have to, because it wasn't ghostie stories. I had Father Maury's things, things that they'd hidden together, for safe keeping, Eoin and Lucie. Hidden in their special place up at the bawn.

It was their secret, Eoin's and Lucie's.

They had hidden the things in Lucie's box, to protect them from the soldiers. Then Eoin was captured and killed, and he died without giving their secret away, and she died without telling. How could she tell? It would have destroyed her father, and she had already hurt him more than enough.

121

The bawn was their special place, where she crept out to meet him from Garrison House.

Now it was over. There'd be no more Ghost Girl, ever.

I was happy for her, and being happy for her made me happy for *me*, as well.

"Canon!" I yelled. "Canon, come here! Come here, Canon, till I show you this!"

POSTSCRIPT

Being an Extract from *A CHRONICLE OF BONECASTLE PARISH, DONEGAL, including an Account of the Arrest and Execution of Father Esmond Maury P.P. in 1744, and the recent recovery of certain documents and artefacts, including Father Maury's crucifix, within the bounds of the Parish,* by Canon Stephen Roche.

". . . clearly, the recent discoveries within the Parish cannot be said to have cleared for all time the charges laid against Father Esmond Maury in the year seventeen hundred and forty four. Nevertheless it must be said that the doubts previously expressed by the present writer and several of Father Maury's contemporaries appear to be supported by what has come to light.

As for the unfortunate Eoin Soraghan of Tomas Mor, little remains to be said. The discovery of Father Maury's crucifix concealed by him in a place of safe keeping within the Parish seems to dispose of the ill judged slanders laid against this man's name. That he took the crucifix to protect it, possibly at the suggestion of Father Maury, is probable. The account in Father Maury's journal of the secret marriage contracted by Eoin with Lucie Murray, daughter of the Garrison Commander, adds poignancy to our understanding of the fate which befell all three in the terrible summer of 1744, when Eoin Soraghan and Father Maury were executed, and Lucie was left alone, unable to share her hopeless grief and confusion with anyone, least of all the father she felt she had betrayed.

The tragedy of Lucie Murray and her father, of Esmond Maury and the spy, Eoin Soraghan, is that their story is commonplace, and their roles appear pre-destined. If they are the victims of Irish History, then so are we . . . but they are dead, and we still have a chance to choose.

We can try to find another way.